Welty, Eudora
  The robber bridegroom.

THE ROBBER BRIDEGROOM

Eudora Welty

Designed and Illustrated by Barry Moser

HARCOURT BRACE JOVANOVICH, PUBLISHERS

San Diego · New York · London

Library of Congress Cataloging-in-Publication Data
Welty, Eudora, 1909–
The robber bridegroom.
I. Moser, Barry. II. Title.
PS3545. E6R6 1987   813'.52   87–21195
ISBN 0–15–178318–7

Printed in the United States of America
First edition
A B C D E

To
Katherine Anne Porter

The Robber Bridegroom

IT WAS THE CLOSE OF DAY WHEN A BOAT TOUCHED
Rodney's Landing on the Mississippi River and
Clement Musgrove, an innocent planter, with a bag
of gold and many presents, disembarked. He had
made the voyage from New Orleans in safety, his
tobacco had been sold for a fair price to the King's men.
In Rodney he had a horse stabled against his return,
and he meant to spend the night there at an inn, for
the way home through the wilderness was beset
with dangers.

As his foot touched shore, the sun sank into the
river the color of blood, and at once a wind sprang up
and covered the sky with black, yellow, and green
clouds the size of whales, which moved across the face
of the moon. The river was covered with foam, and
against the landing the boats strained in the waves and
strained again. River and bluff gave off alike a leaf-
green light, and from the water's edge the red torches
lining the Landing-under-the-Hill and climbing the
bluff to the town stirred and blew to the left and right.

There were sounds of rushing and flying, from the flourish of carriages hurrying through the streets after dark, from the bellowing throats of the flatboatmen, and from the wilderness itself, which lifted and drew itself in the wind, and pressed its savage breath even closer to the little galleries of Rodney, and caused a bell to turn over in one of the steeples, and shook the fort and dropped a tree over the racetrack.

Holding his bag of gold tight in his hand, Clement made for the first inn he saw under the hill. It was all lighted up and full of the sounds of singing.

Clement entered and went straight to the landlord and inquired, "Have you a bed for the night, where I will not be disturbed till morning?"

"Aye," replied the landlord, who brushed at a long mustache—an Englishman.

"But where have you left your right ear?" said Clement, pointing to the vacancy. Like all innocent men, he was proud of having one thing in the world he could be sharp about.

And the landlord was forced to admit that he had left the ear pinned to a market cross in Kentucky, for the horse stealing he did.

Clement turned and went on up the road, and the storm was worse. He asked at the next inn, which was equally glittering and bright, indeed he could not distinguish them in his memory from one year's end to the next, if he might be accommodated for the night.

"Aye," said the landlord, showing his front teeth all of gold.

"But where have you left your left ear?" Clement asked, and he had that man too. The fellow said it had been clipped away in Nashville for the sad trouble he got into after the cockfights.

On he went, the rain worse all the time, until it sounded like the quarreling of wildcats in the cane, and at last, at the very top of the hill, he found an inn where he was able to pronounce the landlord honest.

"Since you appear to be a scrupulous man," he said, "I would like to engage of you a bed for the night, with supper and breakfast, if not too dear."

"To be sure," replied the landlord, the very image of a hare, whose large ears were easily set a-trembling. "But, sir, this is a popular house, if I may say so. You may have one bedfellow, or even two, before the night is over."

At that very moment there came a loud gust of laughter from the grogshop at the side—"Ho! Ho! Ho!"

"But it is early yet," the landlord said, his ears beginning to quiver nonetheless. "If you go up at once, you will be able to take first choice of place in the bed."

Clement stopped only to eat a supper of beefsteak, eggs, bacon, turkey joints, johnnycake, pickled peaches, plum pie, and a bowl of grog before saying good night to him.

"Pleasant dreams!" the landlord said, and the traveler went up the winding stair.

Clement was the first man to the room. The storm was unabated, the wind was shaking the house like a cat a mouse. The rain had turned to hail. First he hid his moneybag under that end of the pillow which was nearest the door, and then he sat down to take off his boots before getting into bed, such being the rule of the house. But before he got his first boot off, in walked a second traveler.

This was a brawny man six and a half feet high, with a blue coat, red shirt, and turkey feather stuck in his cap, and he held a raven on his finger which never blinked an eye, and could say,

> *"Turn back, my bonny,*
> *Turn away home."*

"Ah, stranger," said this fellow to Clement, striding up. "It's been a long time since we slept together."

"So it has," said Clement.

"Have you got the same old smell you had before?" asked the stranger, and Clement did not say no.

"Are you just as lousy as ever?" he roared, and Clement said he was.

"Then shake hands!"

Before Clement could get the second boot off, the third traveler walked in.

He was as brawny as the other, though but six feet tall, and dressed up like a New Orleans dandy, with his short coat knotted about him capewise. But for some reason he wore no hat, and his heavy yellow locks hung over his forehead and down to his shoulders.

"Ah, stranger," said he to the second traveler. "Crowded days! It's been a long time since our heads were side by side on the pillow."

Clement Musgrove

"Long as forever!" sang out the other.

Then Clement knew they were all three strangers to one another, with the stormy night ahead.

When the third traveler removed his cloak, there was a little dirk hid in the knot, which he placed with his moneybag under the pillow. And there were the three bags of gold sitting there side by side, like hens on their nests. So Clement held up the snuffer over the light.

"Wait!" said the third traveler. "Are we dreaming already? We are going off without the last nightcap, gentlemen."

"Ho! Ho! Ho!" said the second traveler, punching himself in the forehead and kicking himself in the breeches. "That is a thing I seldom forget, for my mind is as bright as a gold piece."

All three of them sat and uncorked their jugs and at the same moment drank down. And when they looked up, the second traveler had drunk the whole jugful.

"Remarkable!" said the yellow-haired stranger, who had made way with half a jug. Poor Clement, who had swallowed only a fourth, could say nothing.

"That was only a finicky taste," replied the other, and throwing off his blue coat, he yelled, "Drink again!"

And he seized Clement's own jug out of his finger and emptied it.

"A master!" said Yellowhair. "But I dare say that is the end, the show is over. You can do no more."

"Ho! Ho!" said the other, and taking off his red

shirt and filling his bristling chest with a breath of air, he seized the other's own jug and finished it off.

Then, sailing his cap in the air, he gave a whistle and a shake and declared that he was none other than Mike Fink, champion of all the flatboat bullies on the Mississippi River, and was ready for anything.

"Mike Fink! Well now," said the yellow-haired stranger, and putting his head to one side studied him with all the signs of admiration.

"Yes indeed I am," said the flatboatman crossly. "Am I not Mike Fink, as you live and breathe?" he roared at Clement.

It was a cautious night, but Clement believed him, until the yellow-haired stranger said, "Well, I doubt it."

"You doubt that I am Mike Fink? Nevertheless, it is true!" yelled the flatboatman. "Only look!" And he doubled up his fists and rippled the muscles on his arms up and down, as slow as molasses, and on his chest was the finest mermaid it was possible to have tattooed at any port. "I can pick up a grown man by the neck in each hand and hold him out at arm's length, and often do, too," yelled the flatboatman. "I eat a whole cow at one time, and follow her up with a live sheep if it's Sunday. Ho! ho! If I get hungry on a voyage, I jump off my raft and wade across, and take whatever lies in my path on shore. When I come near, the good folk take to their heels and run from their houses! I only laugh at the Indians, and I can carry a dozen oxen on my back at one time, and as for pigs, I tie them in a bunch and hang them to my belt!"

6

"Strike me dead!" said the yellow-haired stranger, and he yawned, got into bed, and shut his eyes.

"I'm an alligator!" yelled the flatboatman, and began to flail his mighty arms through the air. "I'm a he-bull and a he-rattlesnake and a he-alligator all in one! I've beat up so many flatboatmen and thrown them in the river I haven't kept a count since the flood, and I'm a lover of the women like you'll never see again." And he chanted Mike Fink's song: "I can out-run, outhop, outjump, throw down, drag out, and lick any man in the country!"

"Go down to the corner and buy yourself a new jug," said the yellow-haired stranger. His eyes were shut tight still, though Clement's, you may be sure, were open wide. "You're still nothing but an old buffalo."

"So I lie?" bellowed the flatboatman, and, leaping out of his breeches, he jumped across the room in three jumps and said, "Feast your eyes upon me and deny that I am Mike Fink."

Clement was ready to agree, but the yellow-haired stranger said, "Why, you're nothing but an old hoptoad, you will make me mad in a minute. Now what is it you want? If you want to fight, let us fight."

At that, the flatboatman gave one soul-reaching shout and jumped into the featherbed and burst it, and the yellow-haired stranger leaped up with a laugh, and the feathers blew all around the room like the chips in a waterspout. And out the window it was storming, and from the door the raven was saying,

"Turn again, my bonny,
Turn away home."

As for Clement, he removed himself, since he was a man of peace and would not be wanted on the scene, and held the candle where it would be safe and at the same time cast the best light, and all the while his bedfellows sliced right and left, picked each other up, and threw each other down for a good part of the night. And if he sneezed once, he sneezed a thousand times, for the feathers.

Finally the flatboatman said, "Let us stop and seize forty winks. We will take it up in the morning where we leave off tonight. Agreed?"

"Certainly," said the other, dropping him to the ground where he was about to throw him. "That is the rule Mike Fink would make, if he were here."

"Say once more that I am not Mike Fink and, peace or no peace, that will be your last breath!" cried the flatboatman. And then he said cunningly, "If by now you don't know who I am, *I* know who *you* are, that followed this rich planter to his bed."

"Take care," said the other.

"I will bet all the gold that lies under this pillow against the sickening buttons you wear sewed to your coat, that your name is Jamie Lockhart! Jamie Lock-hart the——"

"Take care," said the other once more, and he half pulled out his little dirk.

"I say for the third time that your name is Jamie Lockhart, the I-forget-what," said the flatboatman.

Mike Fink

"And if that does not make it so, we will leave the decision to this gentleman, whose name has not yet been brought out in the open."

The poor planter could only say, "My name, about which there is no secret, is Clement Musgrove. But I do not know Jamie Lockhart, any more than I know Mike Fink, and will identify neither."

"I am Mike Fink!" yelled the flatboatman. "And that is Jamie Lockhart! And not the other way around, neither! You say you do not know who he is—do you not know *what* he is? He is a——" And he took hold of Clement like a mother bear and waltzed him around, whispering, "Say it! Say it! Say it!"

The poor man began to shake his head with wonder, and he did not like to dance.

But the yellow-haired stranger smiled at him and said coolly enough, "Say *who* I am forever, but dare to say *what* I am, and that will be the last breath of any man."

With that delivered, he lay down in the bed once more, and said to Mike Fink, "Blow out the candle."

The flatboatman immediately closed his mouth, put his breeches and shirt and his coat back on, blew out the candle, and fell into the bed on one side of Jamie Lockhart, if it was he, while the planter, deciding that affairs were at rest for the evening, lay down on the other.

But no sooner had Clement given a groan and got to the first delightful regions of sleep than he felt a hand seize his arm.

"Make no sound, as you value your life," whispered a voice. "But rise up out of the bed."

The storm was over, and the raven was still, but who knows whether he slept? It was the yellow-haired man who had whispered, and Clement had to wonder if now he should find out what Jamie Lockhart was. A murderer? A madman? A ghost? Some outlandish beast in New Orleans dress? He got to his feet and looked at his companion by the pure light of the moon, which by now was shining through the shutter. He was remarkably amiable to see. But by his look, nobody could tell what he would do.

So he led Clement to a corner, and then placed two bundles of sugar cane, that were standing by the wall, in their two places in the bed.

"Why is that?" said Clement.

"Watch and wait," said he, and gave him a flash in the dark from his white teeth.

And in the dead of the night up rose Mike Fink, stretching and giggling, and reaching with his hands he ripped up a long board from out of the floor.

As soon as it came under his touch, he exclaimed in a delighted whisper, "Particle of a flatboat you are! Oh, I would know you anywhere, I'd know you like a woman, I'd know you by your sweet perfume." He gave it a smack and said, "Little piece of flatboat, this is Mike Fink has got you by the tail. Now go to work and ruin these two poor sleeping fools!"

Then he proceeded to strike a number of blows with the plank, dividing them fairly and equally with no favorites between the two bundles of sugar cane lying between the feathers of the bed.

"There! And there! If we have left you one whole bone between you, I'm not the bravest creature in the world and this pretty thing never sprang from a flatboat," he said.

Next, reaching under the tatters of the pillow, he snatched all three bags of gold, like hot johnnycakes from a fire, and lying down and stretching his legs, he went to sleep at once, holding the gold in his two hands against his chest and dreaming about nothing else.

When all was still once more, Clement stretched forth his hand and said, "Are you Jamie Lockhart? I ask your name only in gratitude, and I do not ask you *what* you may be."

"I am Jamie Lockhart," said he.

"How can I thank you, sir, for saving my life?"

"Put it off until morning," said Jamie Lockhart. "For now, as long as we are supposed to be dead, we can sleep in peace."

He and the planter then fell down and slept until cockcrow.

Next morning Clement awoke to see Jamie Lockhart up and in his boots. Jamie gave him a signal, and he hid with him in the wardrobe and watched out through the crack.

So Mike Fink woke up with a belch like the roar of a lion.

"Next day!" announced Mike, and he jumped out

of bed. With a rousing clatter the moneybags fell off his chest to the floor. "Gold!" he cried. Then he bent down and counted it, every piece, and then, as if with a sudden recollection, he stirred around in the bed with his finger, although he held his other hand over his eyes and would not look. "Nothing left of the two of them but the juice," said he.

Then Jamie Lockhart gave Clement a sign, and out they marched from the wardrobe, not saying a thing.

The flatboatman fell forward as if the grindstone were hung about his neck.

"Bogeys!" he cried.

"Good morning! Could this be Mike Fink?" inquired Jamie Lockhart politely.

"Holy Mother! Bogeys for sure!" he cried again.

"Don't you remember Jamie Lockhart, or has it been so long ago?"

"Oh, Jamie Lockhart, how do you feel?"

"Fine and fit."

"Did you sleep well?"

"Yes indeed," said Jamie, "except for some rats which slapped me with their tails once or twice in the night. Did you notice it, Mr. Musgrove?"

"Yes," said Clement, by the plan, "now that I think of it."

"I do believe they were dancing a Natchez Cotillion on my chest," said Jamie.

And at that the flatboatman cried "Bogeys!" for the last time, and jumped out the window. There he

Jamie Lockhart

had left three sacks of gold behind him, Clement Musgrove's, Jamie Lockhart's and his own.

"Gone for good," said Jamie. "And so we will have to get rid of his gold somehow."

"Please be so kind as to dispose of that yourself," Clement said, "for my own is enough for me, and I have no interest in it."

"Very well," said he, "though it is the talking bird that takes my fancy more."

"You may have that and welcome. And now tell me what thing of mine you will accept, for you saved my life," said the planter in great earnestness.

Jamie Lockhart smiled and said, "I stand in need of one thing, it is true, and without it I may even be in danger of arrest."

"What is that?"

"A Spanish passport. It is only a formality, and a small matter, but I am a stranger in the Natchez country. It requires a recommendation to the Governor by a landowner like yourself."

"I will give it gladly," said Clement. "Before you go, I will write it out. But tell me—will you settle hereabouts?"

"Perhaps," said Jamie, making ready to go. "That is yet to be seen. Yet we shall surely meet again," he said, knotting the sleeves of his coat about his shoulders and taking up the bird on his left forefinger. It said at once, as though there it belonged,

> *"Turn back, my bonny,*
> *Turn away home."*

Clement decided then and there to invite this man to dine with him that very Sunday night. But first, being a gullible man, one given to trusting all listening people, Clement sat Jamie Lockhart down in the Rodney inn, looked him kindly in the face, and told him the story of his life.

"I was once married to a beautiful woman of Virginia," he said, "her name was Amalie. We lived in the peaceful hills. The first year, she bore me two blissful twins, a son and a daughter, the son named for me and the daughter named Rosamond. And it was not long before we set out with a few of the others, and were on our way down the river. That was the beginning of it all," said Clement, "the journey down. On the flatboat around our fire we crouched and looked at one another—I, my first wife Amalie, Kentucky Thomas and his wife Salome, and the little twins like cubs in their wrappings. The reason I ever came is forgotten now," he said. "I know I am not a seeker after anything, and ambition in this world never stirred my heart once. Yet it seemed as if I was caught up by what came over the others, and they were the same. There was a great tug at the whole world, to go down over the edge, and one and all we were changed into pioneers, and our hearts and our own lonely wills may have had nothing to do with it."

"Don't go fretting over the reason," said Jamie kindly, "for it may have been the stars."

"The stars shone down on all our possessions," said Clement, "as if they were being counted and found a small number. The stars shone brightly—too brightly. We could see too well then not to drift onward, too well to tie up and keep the proper vigil. At some point under the stars, the Indians lured us to shore."

"How did they do it?" asked Jamie. "What trick did they use? The savages are so clever they are liable to last out, no matter how we stamp upon them."

"The Indians know their time has come," said Clement. "They are sure of the future growing smaller always, and that lets them be infinitely gay and cruel. They showed their pleasure and their lack of surprise well enough, when we climbed and crept up to them as they waited on all fours, disguised in their bearskins and looking as fat as they could look, out from the head of the bluff."

"They took all your money, of course," said Jamie. "And I wonder how much it was you would have had to give. Only yesterday I heard of a case where travelers captured in the wilderness gave up three hundred doubloons, seventy-five bars of gold in six-by-eights, five hundred French guineas, and any number of odd pieces, the value of which you could not tell without weighing them—all together about fifteen thousand dollars."

But if he spoke a hint, Clement did not hear it. "The money was a little part," he said. "In their camp where we were taken—a clear-swept, devious, aromatic place under flowering trees—we were encircled and made to perform and go naked like slaves. We had to go whirling and dizzied in a dance we had never suspected lay in our limbs. We had to be humiliated and tortured and enjoyed, and finally, with the most precise formality, to be decreed upon. All of them put on their blazing feathers and stood looking us down as if we were little mice."

"This must have been long ago," said Jamie. "For they are not so fine now, and cannot do so much to prisoners as that."

"The son named after me was dropped into a pot of burning oil," said Clement, "and my wife Amalie fell dead out of the Indians' arms before the sight. This made the Indians shiver with scorn; they thought she should have lived on where she stood. In their contempt they turned me free, and put a sort of mark upon me. There is nothing that you can see, but something came out of their eyes. Kentucky Thomas was put to death. Then I, who had shed tears, and my child, that was a girl, and Salome, the ugly woman they were all afraid of, were turned into the wilderness, bound together. They beat us out with their drums."

"The Indians wanted you to be left with less than nothing," said Jamie.

"Like other devices tried upon a man's life, this could have compelled love," Clement said. "I walked tied beside this woman Salome, carrying my child, hungry and exhausted and in hiding for longer than I remember."

"And now she is your second wife," said Jamie, "and you have prospered, have you not?"

"From the first, Salome turned her eyes upon me with less question than demand, and that is the most impoverished gaze in the world. There was no longer

Salome Musgrove

anything but ambition left in her destroyed heart. We scarcely spoke to each other, but each of us spoke to the child. As I grew weaker, she grew stronger, and flourished by the struggle. She could have taken her two hands and broken our bonds apart, but she did not. I never knew her in any of her days of gentleness, which must have been left behind in Kentucky. The child cried, and she hushed it in her own way. One morning I said to myself, 'If we find a river, let that be a sign, and I will marry this woman,' but I did not think we would ever find a river. Then almost at once we came upon it—the whole Mississippi. A priest coming down from Tennessee on a flatboat to sell his whisky stopped when he saw us, cut us loose from each other, then married us. He fed us meat, blessed us, gave us a gallon of corn whisky, and left us where we were."

"And you turned into a planter on the spot," said Jamie, "and I wonder how much you are worth now!"

"There on the land which the King of Spain granted to me," said Clement, bent to tell his full story now or burst, "I built a little hut to begin with. But when my first tobacco was sold at the market, Salome, my new wife, entreated me in the night to build a better house, like the nearest settler's, and so I did. There was added the fine bedroom with a mirror to hang on the wall, and after the bedroom a separate larder, and behind the house a kitchen with a great oven. And behind the kitchen in a little pen was a brand-new pig, and tied beyond him to a tree was a fresh cow. A big black dog barked in the dooryard to keep anybody out, and a cock jumped on the roof of the house every morning and crowed loud enough to alarm the whole country.

"'How is this, wife?' said I.

"'We shall see,' Salome said. 'For it is impossible not to grow rich here.'"

"And she was right," said Jamie.

"Yes, she was right," Clement said. "She would stand inflexible and tireless, casting long black shadows from the candle she would be always carrying about the halls at night. She was never certain that we lived unmolested, and examined the rooms without satisfaction. Often she carried a rifle in the house, and she still does. You would see her eyes turn toward any open door, as true as a wheel. I brought her many gifts, more and more, that she would take out of their wrappings without a word and lay away in a chest."

"A woman to reckon with, your second wife," said Jamie with a musing smile.

Clement closed his lips then, but he remembered how in her times of love Salome was immeasurably calculating and just so, almost clocklike, in the way of the great Spanish automaton in the iron skirt in the New Orleans bazaar, which could play and beat a man at chess.

"As soon as possible," said Clement aloud, "I would bring her another present, to stop the guilt in my heart."

"Guilt is a burdensome thing to carry about in the heart," said Jamie. "I would never bother with it."

"Then you are a man of action," said Clement, "a man of the times, a pioneer and a free agent. There is no one to come to you saying 'I want' what you do not want. 'Clement,' Salome would say, 'I want a gig to drive in to Rodney.' 'Let us wait another year,' said I. 'Nonsense!' So there would be a gig. Next, 'Clement, I want a row of silver dishes to stand on the shelf.' 'But my dear wife, how can we be sure of the food to go in them?' And the merchants, you know, have us at their mercy. Nevertheless, my next purchase off the Liverpool ship was not a new wrought-iron plow, but the silver dishes. And it did seem that whatever I asked of the land I planted on I would be given, when she told me to ask, and there was no limit to its favors."

"How is your fortune now?" asked Jamie, leaning forward on his two elbows.

"Well, before long a little gallery with four posts appeared across the front of my house, and we were sitting there in the evening; and new slaves sent out with axes were felling more trees, and indigo and tobacco were growing nearer and nearer to the river there under the black shadow of the forest. Then in one of the years she made me try cotton, and my fortune was made. I suppose that at the moment," said Clement in conclusion, but with no show of confidence (for to tell the truth, he was not sure exactly what he was worth), "I may be worth thousands upon thousands of gold pieces."

"You are a successful man," said Jamie, "willy-nilly."

"But on some of the mornings as I ride out," said Clement, "my daughter Rosamond runs and stops me on the path and says, 'Father, why was it you shouted out so loudly in the night?' And I tell her that

I had a dream. 'What was your dream?' says she. 'In the dream, whenever I lie down, then it is the past. When I climb to my feet, then it is the present. And I keep up a struggle not to fall.' And Rosamond says, 'It is my own mother you love, swear it is so.' And Salome listens at the doors and I hear her say to herself, 'I had better wake him each morning just before his dream, which comes at dawn, and declare my rights.'" Clement sighed and said, "It is want that does the world's arousing, and if it were not for that, who knows what might not be interrupted?"

But Jamie said he must go, and reminded him of the passport that was needed.

"You have interested me very much," said Clement, when he had written it out; for the poor man was under the misapprehension that he now knew everything about Jamie, instead of seeing the true fact that Jamie now knew everything about him. "And in order to persuade you to settle near-by, and come and talk more to me in the evenings, I invite you to dine with me on next Sunday night. It is only three hours' ride away, and I will meet you here to show you the way."

"And I think I will come," said Jamie, his teeth flashing in a smile. But his look was strange indeed.

"I wish to introduce you," said Clement, nevertheless, "to Salome; and to my daughter Rosamond, who is so beautiful that she keeps the memory of my first wife alive and evergreen in my heart."

Then they both rode away—Clement through the wilderness to his plantation, and Jamie on an errand of his own, with the raven perched on his shoulder.

2

Away out in the woods from rodney's land-ing, in a clearing in the live-oaks and the cedars and the magnolia trees, with the Mississippi River a mile to the back and the Old Natchez Trace a mile to the front, was the house Clement Musgrove had built that had grown from a hut, and there was the smoke now coming out the chimney. So while he was riding home through the wilderness, there in the kitchen was his wife Salome, stirring a ladle in a pot of brew, and there at the window above was his daughter Rosamond, leaning out to sing a song which floated away on the air.

Rosamond was truly a beautiful golden-haired girl, locked in the room by her stepmother for singing, and still singing on, because it passed the time away better than anything else. This was the way the song began:

"The moon shone bright, and it cast a fair light:
'Welcome,' says she, 'my honey, my sweet!
For I have loved thee this seven long year,
And our chance it was we could never meet.'

Then he took her in his armes-two,
And kissed her both cheek and chin,
And twice or thrice he kissed this may
Before they were parted in twin."

Before Rosamond came to the end of this love ballad, which was meant to be very long, Salome unlocked the door and there she stood like an old blackbird.

"Well, lazy thing," said she, "I need fresh herbs for the pot. There are some extra-large ones growing on the other side of the woods at the farthest edge of the indigo field. Go and pick them and don't come back till your apron is full."

And for a thing like this she would send Rosamond out alone every morning while her father was away, when he knew nothing of it. She would think that perhaps the Indians might kidnap the girl and adopt her into their tribe, and give her another name, or that a leopard might walk out between two trees and carry her off in his teeth before she could say a word.

For if Rosamond was as beautiful as the day, Salome was as ugly as the night, and all her gnashing of teeth made her none the better-looking.

So Rosamond said, "Yes, stepmother," and taking

the time to dress herself in a light blue gown, bind her hair with a ribbon, and bake herself a little hoecake for a lunch, she made ready for her expedition.

"If you come back without the herbs, I'll break your neck," said the stepmother. "Now be gone!"

Rosamond on her way had to pass through a little locust grove, and as she walked underneath the boughs where the wild bees were humming, she always took hold of her mother's locket, which she wore on a silver chain, and the locket would seem to speak of its own accord. What it never failed to say was, "If your mother could see you now, her heart would break."

On she went then, and no sooner was she out of sight under the trees than up to the door rode Clement coming home on his horse. Salome had sent the girl away in the nick of time, and indeed she had had her eyes upon her husband since he was no more than a speck of dust, to see if she could tell from a distance what presents he was bringing; and she wanted to get · her own name on the best ones.

Clement came in, and the first thing he said was, "Hello, wife, where is my little daughter gone?" for she had not run out to meet him, and that was as if the jessamines had not bloomed that year.

"Oh, she is safe enough, I have no doubt, and has forgotten us entirely," replied Salome, with a smile on her face all its own. "Her idleness has led her out of the house again, out dressed in her best, fit to meet the King there in the nettles, and not a word behind her of where she was going. Here I am keeping her dinner warm over the fire." For this was the way she would talk to her husband.

"My poor little daughter!" said Clement sadly. "It is a good thing that I married the woman who would look after my child," he said to himself, "or what would happen to her then?"

Then Salome gritted her teeth, but she saved up on her anger to vent it in some grand way later, when the time was sure to come.

"How much did you get for your tobacco, and where are the presents you were to bring?" she said next.

"Here are the moneybags, count it for yourself when the table is cleared," said Clement, who would not cheat even a little midge of its pleasures. "And here is the packet of needles, the paper of pins, length of calico, pair of combs, orange, Madeira, and muscadine wine, the salt for the table, and all from the apothecary that he could provide."

"And is the silk gown for me too?" Salome asked, paying no heed to the rest but holding up to herself a beautiful dress the green of the sugar cane, and looking like an old witch dressed up for a christening.

"No, that is not for you, but for Rosamond," said Clement. "And so are the hairpins, and the petticoat stitched all around with golden thread, the like of which the young ladies are wearing in New Orleans."

"As if she were not vain enough as it is!" cried Salome. "And now these fancy things will be putting thoughts into her head, you mark my words, and away she will run, off with some river rat, like Livvie

Rosamond Musgrove

Lane and her sister Lambie on the next plantation, there within a week of each other."

Then Rosamond came back, with an apron full of herbs for the pot, and tried on the dress and the petticoat both before she would eat. What a sight she was! She pinned up her hair and she swept up and down the puncheon floor swaying like a swan, and flung her train about.

And the moment she saw Rosamond in the new clothes, Salome's heart felt like lead, and she had no more peace day or night.

"What have you been doing while I was gone?" said Clement when Rosamond had flung her arms around his neck to thank him, for she had never suspected that he would bring her anything except a childish and harmless toy.

"Oh, every day I go to the farthest edge of the indigo field, on the other side of the woods, and gather the herbs that grow there," said Rosamond, "for my stepmother will have no other kind. And today a little old panther came out from behind a holly tree and rubbed up against my side. I took him in my arms, to see what he would do, and he gave me a little purr. Just then the mother panther let go from the tree above my head, and down she lit on her feet, stirring up the leaves like a whirlwind and growling from end to end, like the gold organ in the Rodney church. She was ten feet long and she must have been nine feet high when her hair started rising, for she reached away over my head when I looked her up and down. The first thing I knew she took me up in her teeth, but very

27

easy, by the sash, and carried me all the way home through the woods before she set me down at the gate. She swung me hard, and I knew she meant it for a lesson, and so I came away from her, and here I am, but the whole time I never dropped the leaf of one herb."

Now Rosamond was a great liar, and nobody could believe a word she said. But it took all the starch out of the stepmother, you can be sure, to send Rosamond out on a dangerous errand, hoping some ill might befall her, and then to have her come safely back with a tale of something even worse than she had wished upon her. As for Rosamond, she did not mean to tell anything but the truth, but when she opened her mouth in answer to a question, the lies would simply fall out like diamonds and pearls. Her father had tried scolding her, and threatening to send her away to the Female Academy, and then marching her off without her supper, but none of it had done any good, and so he let her alone. Now and then he remarked that if a man could be found anywhere in the world who could make her tell the truth, he would turn her over to him. Salome, on the other hand, said she should be given a dose of Dr. Peachtree.

"Next year, perhaps, she will submit to a tutor," said Clement to Salome, "and learn Greek and sewing and the guitar."

"Never! I will learn it all for myself," said poor Rosamond, and picking up the guitar, sure enough, she played "Fair as the Rose."

Near Clement's house, down in a gully, lived a poor widow and her six gawky daughters and her only son. The son, who was the youngest, was named Goat, because he could butt his way out the door when his mother left him locked in, and equally, because he could butt his way in when she left him locked out. Every time she would go off, and tell him to be sure not to stir from the house while she was gone, to any wrestling matches, horse races, gander pullings, shooting matches, turkey shoots, or cockfights whatever in Rodney, or she would knock his head off with the skillet, she would be sure to find him missing when she got back. And this in spite of all her promises to bring him presents, and so it was useless to bring him any. Goat was full of curiosity, and anything he found penned up he would let out, including himself. He had let loose all the little colts and pigs and calves and the flocks of geese, peahens, chickens, and turkeys in that part of the country, and he would let anything out of a trap, if he had to tear its leg off to do it.

Now by some manner and the way things come about, Salome had found a familiar in little Goat, and it was there in the back of her head to use him for her own ends. She could not buy him for a slave, because he was not in any degree a black African, but she took the old mother a quart jar of pickled peaches she had put up with her own hands, and looked so grand, that the mother freely gave her Goat for whatever occasion he was wanted, just so she got him back.

So the very next day after Clement brought Rosamond the silk dress like the dresses the Creole girls wore, and Salome's heart was getting no lighter but as heavy as iron, down crept the old stepmother behind the house into the gully and called away at Goat.

Goat, who had been left by the coals to watch a johnnycake, came out through a hole in the door with his hair all matted up and the color of carrots, and his two eyes so crossed they looked like one. He smiled and he had every other tooth, but that was all. He stood there with his two big toes sticking up.

"I hope you are well, Goat," said Salome, giving her own brand of smile, and Goat said he had never felt better, as far as he could recollect.

"You remember that you are working for me, don't you, Goat?" said Salome.

"Yes indeed," said Goat, "until a better offer comes along."

"Then here is your work for today," said Salome, and she bent down as close to him as she dared, for he could have bitten her, and whispered a rigmarole into his ear.

"Leave it to me," said Goat afterwards. "You have not spoken to a deaf man."

So they sealed a bargain and Salome crept home to sit and wait.

In the meanwhile, Rosamond was fastening on her clothes, and she was putting on the new silk gown, for she was determined never again to wear any other. She pinned up her long hair with the pins. Then just as she was getting a look into the mirror, in walked Salome like a shadow across the sun.

Goat

"Well, my fine lady, I need herbs for the pot, for all that you got yesterday have lost their power today," she said. "Pick me nothing but the fine ones growing on the other side of the woods at the farthest edge of the indigo field. And don't dare to come home till you have filled your apron."

"Oh, but that will ruin my dress," cried poor Rosamond.

"That is because you are fool enough to wear it," said the stepmother, and so Rosamond had to go, and the stepmother called after her, "If you come back without the herbs, I'll wring your neck!"

Rosamond passed again through the little locust grove, and heard the golden hum of the bees, and took hold of the little locket. The locket spoke and said, "If your mother could see you now, her heart would break."

Then on she went, and this time, skulking along behind her, but well out of sight, was Goat, bent on his task and thinking as hard as he could so as not to forget it.

First Rosamond went through the woods and then she passed along the field of indigo, and finally she came to the very edge, which was by the side of a deep, dark ravine. And at the foot of this ravine ran the Old Natchez Trace, that old buffalo trail where travelers passed along and were set upon by the bandits and the Indians and torn apart by the wild animals.

There were the thorns and briars and among them the green herbs growing. No matter how many Rosamond picked, they always seemed to be just as thick the next day. So Rosamond held up her fine silk skirt and threw the herbs into it as she picked.

Now all this time, Goat had been keeping the little distance behind Rosamond, looking for his chance to finish her off. Those had been his directions in the long rigmarole Salome had whispered in his ear. If Rosamond were to take a look over the ravine's edge, he was to give her the right push, and if she were to fall into one of the bear traps he was to stop up his ears and not let her loose. And if anything whatever chanced to happen to her, he had only to remember to bring back a bit of her dress, all torn and rubbed in the dust, as a sign she was surely dead, and he would get his reward, a suckling pig.

Rosamond went about her business of gathering herbs, and if she saw or heard anything of Goat in the bush, she thought it was an Indian or a wildcat and paid no attention to it; for she was wearing her mother's locket, which kept her from the extravagant harms of the world and only let her in for the little ones.

It was not long before she opened her mouth and sang,

> "The moon shone bright, and it cast a fair light:
> 'Welcome,' says she, 'my honey, my sweet!
> For I have loved thee this seven long year,
> And our chance it was we could never meet.'"

And although she had never loved or known any man except her father, her voice was so sad and so sweet and full of love itself that Goat was on the very point of tears in the bushes.

No sooner had she finished the first verse of the song when there was a pounding of hoof beats on the Trace below, and along under the crossed branches of the trees came riding none other than Jamie Lockhart, out for a devilment of some kind, with his face all stained in berry juice for a disguise.

When he heard Rosamond singing so sweetly, as if she had been practicing just for this, he had to look up, and as soon as he saw her he turned his horse straight up the bank and took it in three leaps.

"Good morning," said he, getting off his horse, a red stallion named Orion, which at once began to graze upon the fine herbs growing under his nose.

"Good morning," said Rosamond, and she was so surprised that she let her skirt fall, and all the herbs she had gathered scattered to the wind.

"That is a grand dress you are wearing out for nothing," said Jamie, with a look coming into his eye.

"All my dresses are like this one," said Rosamond. "Only this is the worst of the lot, and that is why I don't care what happens to it."

"How lucky you are today, then, my girl," said Jamie, giving her a flash of his white teeth. "So put off the clothes you're wearing now, for I'm taking them with me."

"And who told you you might ask me for them?" cried Rosamond.

"No one tells me and no one needs to tell me," said

33

Jamie, "for I am a bandit and I think of everything for myself."

And he led her by the hand into a clump of green willows, where they would not be seen by other travelers or bandits coming along the Trace.

"So pull your dress off over your head, my bonny, for you'll not go a step further with it on," he said.

"Well, then, I suppose I must give you the dress," said Rosamond, "but not a thing further."

"Oh!" spoke up Goat, where he was hiding behind the bush. "It's a shame now to take that off, for the petticoat is much too beautiful beneath."

But Rosamond was so busy with the little pins, which she took care to stick back in the dress, that she could not hear.

Then she stood before Jamie in the wonderful petticoat stitched all around with golden thread, and at once he must have that too.

"Put off your petticoat," he said, "for the dish requires the sauce."

The tears sprang for a moment to Rosamond's eyes, and she said to herself, "If my mother knew I had to give up the petticoat as well, her heart would break."

"Oh!" cried Goat from his hiding place, "never give up the spangled petticoat, for you are far too beautiful beneath!"

But at that moment Rosamond was so particular not to catch the tassels on the thorns that she never heard a thing.

Then she stood in front of Jamie in her cotton petticoats two deep, and he said, "Off with the smocks, girl, and be quick."

"Are you leaving me nothing?" cried Rosamond, darting glances all about her for help, but there wasn't any to be had, though Goat looked about too.

"I am taking some and all away with me," said Jamie. "Off with the rest."

"God help me," said Rosamond, who had sometimes imagined such a thing happening, and knew what to say. "Were you born of a woman? For the sake of your poor mother, who may be dead in her grave, like mine, I pray you to leave me with my underbody."

"Yes, I was born of a woman," said Jamie, "but for no birth that she bore or your mother bore either will I leave you with so much as a stitch, for I am determined to have all."

So Rosamond took off the first smock. "You may not know," said she, "that I have a father who has killed a hundred Indians and twenty bandits as well, and seven brothers that are all in hearty health. They will come after you for this, you may be sure, and hang you to a tree before you are an hour away."

"I will take all eight as they come, then," said Jamie, and he took out his airy little dirk. "Off with the last item," he said, "for I must hurry if a father and seven sons are waiting for the chase."

"Oh!" said Goat from the bush. "You are done for now, and my work is finished, and I might as well go home."

But Rosamond, who had imagined such things happening in the world, and what she would do if they did, reached up and pulled the pins out of her hair, and down fell the long golden locks, almost to the ground, but not quite, for she was very young yet. And as for hearing the sighs of little Goat, she was thinking of how ever she might look without a stitch on her, and would not have heard a thunderclap.

"Thank you, now," said Jamie, gathering up all the clothes from the grass and not forgetting the gold hairpins from France that were scattered about. "But wait," he said, "which would you rather? Shall I kill you with my little dirk, to save your name, or will you go home naked?"

"Oh," cried Goat, "you are done for either way, but if you let him kill you now I will get a suckling pig."

"Why, sir, life is sweet," said Rosamond, looking up straight at him through the two curtains of her hair, "and before I would die on the point of your sword, I would go home naked any day."

"Then good-by," said Jamie, and leaping on his horse and crying "Success!", away he went, leaving her standing there.

When Rosamond reached home, the sun was straight up in the sky, and there were her father and stepmother sitting on either side of the front door in their chairs.

Salome said, "Rosamond, speak! Where are the pot-herbs I sent you for?"

But her father said, "In God's name, the child is as naked as a jay bird."

And he took hold of her and asked her what in the name of heaven had befallen her.

Rosamond, naked

"Well, I will tell you," said Rosamond.

But first her father put over her his planter's coat, which doused her like a light, and said, "Before you begin, remember that truth is brief, for if you lie now, you will catch your death of a chill." And her step-mother's ears were opening like morning-glories to the sun.

Rosamond began and said, "Every day, I go to the farthest edge of the indigo field, on the other side of the woods, to gather the herbs that grow there, for my stepmother will have no other kind."

"Yes, yes," said poor Clement, "but make haste with the story."

"So on this day," said Rosamond, "I was gathering the herbs into my skirt and singing this song:

"'Oh the moon shone bright, and it cast a fair light:
"Welcome," says she, "my honey, my sweet——"'"

"Never mind all the verses now," said Clement. "Skip over to the end."

"Well, in the end, there came the bandit," said Rosamond, "riding his horse up the Old Natchez Trace. He was a very tall bandit with berry stains on his face so that nobody could tell what he looked like or who he was. His horse was as red as fire, and set to work right away biting off the tops of the herbs."

"Yes, no doubt," said Clement. "But hurry on with the news. The truth is longer than I thought."

"So he said 'Good morning,' and I said 'Good morning.' And I was so surprised to see him so polite that I dropped my skirt to the ground and all the herbs fell out, and that is why I did not bring them home."

"A likely excuse!" said Salome, and her eye traveled round to look for Goat, and her two hands went into fists to take him by the heels and shake his story out.

"What next, after the salutations?" poor Clement begged. "For something must go on from there, and this is the time I dread to hear what it was."

"Next, the bandit said, 'That's a grand dress you are wearing out for nothing,' for alas, I had on the New Orleans dress," said Rosamond, "and Father, for this, I never deserve to have another."

And her father said "Alas" too, for now he was going to hear what had happened to it.

"Well," said Rosamond, "the long and short of it is that the bandit took it, and took not only my dress but my petticoat with the golden tassels, my cotton petticoats, and, although I asked him in his mother's name to refrain, my underbody."

"And did he leave you then?" cried Clement.

"He left me then," said Rosamond, "though I had not been sure what he would do, my hair, brushed every night as it is, still being of uncertain length when I let it down."

And at first they did not believe her, but by dark she had told it the same way at least seven times, until there was nothing else to do but believe her, unless they jumped down the well.

"Where did the bastard go?" cried Clement, jumping to his feet the moment he was convinced, "for I will follow him and string him to a tree for this."

"I gave him my word that you would indeed, Father," said Rosamond, "but he replied that there was no hope for you to saddle your horse for that, since he was aiming to cross the river into the wilds of Louisiana, where you could never get at him."

Nevertheless, Clement saddled his horse and rode all night, looking for the bandit, and finding nothing but the dark and cold.

But to Salome he said, "There is a thing the bandit did not count on, and it is this: I know the man to catch him where I cannot, the man who has the brains and the bravery and the very passport to do it. And that is Jamie Lockhart, the man who saved my life at the Rodney inn, and the very man to avenge my daughter's honor as well."

"But how do we know your daughter retains her honor?" asked Salome, gritting her teeth at the very thought of rescue. "Bandits, panthers, and the like indeed! The panther carries her gently in his teeth, and sets her down without harm, and the bandit robs her of every stitch she has on, and leaves her untouched. It is something to meditate about, my good husband!"

"Hold your tongue, woman!" cried Clement, full of anger, and for once he wondered if the stepmother really loved his little girl. Something seemed to fill the air like a black cloud, and the house shook as if from thunder.

When Rosamond appeared, dressed in her old

blue gown, Clement asked her for the last time if she was quite sure she had not fallen into the bayou and gotten her dress wet, so that she had to leave it to dry there on the bank, with all her petticoats, and if they might not be there still.

But Rosamond said, "No, Father, it was a bandit that took them, and all just as I told you."

So Clement said, "Sunday night, which is tomorrow, I am bringing Jamie Lockhart to search out and kill this bandit of the woods. But in the meanwhile, stay away from the place where the pot-herbs grow, and never go there again. For next time, the bandit may do worse."

But Rosamond only opened the window and sang a song which floated away on the bright blue air.

Now back in the herb patch, Goat had seen everything and lost track of nothing. But at the final point, seeing Rosamond separated from her clothes, he had had to make his mind up which to follow, and he had decided upon the clothes. It was evident that the clothes had cost money and Rosamond had not, and he was influenced by the bandit's choice in the matter as well. And besides, Goat knew better than not to place his hand before his eyes in the presence of naked ladies, or he would get the pillory, and that way he would have been sure to fall in the briars going home.

The bandit had galloped away like the wind and was a flicker on the hill, so Goat made haste to start off in that direction. He followed along up the Natchez

Trace, keeping his eye out for the dress, and once he thought he saw it floating on the creek, but it was only the lily pads, and once he thought he saw it flying in the sky, but then he heard a distant moo, and it was only the old flying cow of Mobile going by. So eventually, after a day of starvation, he turned around and came back home.

The door was locked, but he butted his way into the kitchen and took up a loaf from the shovel and put it in his mouth.

"Hello, Mother," he said, "here I am back."

"Oh, cark and care," said his mother. "Did you bring any money?"

"No," he said, "but I have only to ask the rich lady for it, for I am doing a job of work for her and she is in debt to me."

"Are you sure she is rich," said the mother, "since she has paid you nothing?"

"All the surer," said Goat. "Rich she is, and a good thing for her, for she's as tall as a house, as dark as down a well, and as old as the hills, with such a face that's enough to make anybody die laughing or crying to see it, if they had nothing else to do."

"Then you'll do well to get your money from her," said the mother. "And get it in a hurry, or I'll brain you with the skillet for being so little comfort to me in my old age."

"I'm on my way now, as soon as I hear the news," said Goat. "What's the cry? Are my six sisters married off yet?"

"No more than they were before or ever will be," said the mother, "without a cent in the world to go with them."

"Well, you have only to wait till I bring the money home to see how the money works," said Goat. "Tell all six virgins to come in and brighten themselves up a little. Pack up their clothes, sit them on their chairs, and wait for my return."

So he was off up the hill and gave a whistle, and Salome came out in her hood and led him to the pear orchard, where the branches raining down to the ground hid them from sight.

"Well," said she, "did you follow her?"

"Like the lamb to school," said Goat.

"You saw it all?"

"I gave myself but one blink of the eye," said Goat.

"Then what of the moment when she stood there naked?" asked Salome, ready to burst for wanting to know.

"Oh, I shut my eyes for that," said Goat, whirling in a circle before her black frown. "For they'll never put me in the pillory for *you* to bail out."

"Why don't I kill you?" cried Salome furiously. "Ass! Fool! Then did you follow her still? What was the path she took home?"

"I followed the girl until she and the dress separated and took opposite ways," said Goat. "And since he chose the dress, I chose the dress, and went off hot after that, but it got away. Yet I recall one place now where I haven't looked, and that is in your bear trap."

"Fool!" cried Salome. "It is the girl I sent you to

follow, and now the thing has happened which I looked for to happen, and you were blinking your eye! You have robbed me of my satisfaction, and robbed me of my proof. Idiot! Begone!" For she knew how to talk to Goat just like his own mother.

"First I would like my pay," said Goat.

"Here, take it then," said Salome, and she began boxing him well about the ears.

"That's enough," said Goat, "for I did not work quite that hard."

"One more chance will I give you," said Salome. "I think the girl will go out again in the morning. Follow her and never let her out of your sight. And whatever transpires, remember it as if it were written down and you could read, and come back and tell me."

"Consider it done," said Goat, and at once he jumped in a bush to hide.

Early the next morning, before the sun was up, the stepmother waked Rosamond and shook her till her bones rattled.

"Out of your bed, lazy girl," she said. "Your father has left already to ride to Rodney's Landing. He's buying the whisky, from Father O'Connell, for Jamie Lockhart to drink tonight when he brings him home for supper, and he's left you in my charge. So get up and milk the cows."

"Why should the slaves not milk the cows, for they do it every day and I have never done it before," said Rosamond, for it seemed to her that she had not got her dream dreamed out.

43

"Silence!" cried the stepmother. "I am punishing you, you stupid thing, for what happened yesterday. Have you forgotten already?"

So Rosamond got out of her bed, and while she was brushing her hair and tying it up, the stepmother made off with the little locket on the silver chain which had belonged to the girl's own mother, and Rosamond never missed it. Then Salome hurried away to her room hunched like an old rabbit over her prize.

Rosamond dressed and said her prayers and then she was out of the house and in the paddock milking the cows. But she found she did not mind it at all; for the creatures allowed her to lean her head against their soft foreheads, where their horns stood shining like the crescent moon, and they put out their warm tongues on her cheek, and not a one of them kicked her over for not knowing how a cow is milked, but let her go on with it in her own way.

When the rooster was crowing from the rooftop, Rosamond came round the house carrying the pail with the sound of the foam in it. The smell of night had not yet returned to the woods; and there was a star shining in the daylight. The gate was there at Rosamond's hand, and she touched it and it opened, and she went through; and up at the window was something dark looking down, her stepmother or the cat.

Rosamond found herself before she knew it at the edge of the forest, and with the next step the house was out of sight. And she was still carrying the pail of milk in her hand.

It was so early that the green was first there, then not there in the treetops, but green seemed to beat on the air like a pulse. Once a redbird gave a call, for he too had been waked up in the dark, and had been purely compelled to sing this one note before the prism light of day would divert it into the old song. But Rosamond was not led by him to sing for herself, and only walked on and on into the woods.

The next sounds she heard were distant hoof-beats, lapping like the river waves against the sunrise. It was Jamie Lockhart coming on red Orion, the same as he had been before, in his robber's rags. He rode right up to her, and reached down his arms and lifted her up, pail of milk and all, into the saddle with scarcely a pause in his speed.

Up the ridge they went, and a stream of mist made a circle around them. Then it unwound and floated below in the hollows. The dark cedars sprang from the black ravine, the hanging fruit trees shone ahead on their crests and were hidden again by the cedars. The morning sky rolled slowly like a dark wave they were overtaking, but it had the sound of thunder. Over and over, the same hill seemed to rise beneath the galloping horse. Over and under was another sound, like horses following—was it her father, or an echo?—faster and faster, as they rode the faster.

Rosamond's hair lay out behind her, and Jamie's hair was flying too. The horse was the master of everything. He went like an arrow with the distance behind him and the dark wood closing together. On

Rosamond's arm was the pail of milk, and yet so smoothly did they travel that not a single drop was spilled. Rosamond's cloak filled with wind, and then in the one still moment in the middle of a leap, it broke from her shoulder like a big bird, and dropped away below. Red as blood the horse rode the ridge, his mane and tail straight out in the wind, and it was the fastest kidnaping that had ever been in that part of the country.

Birds flew up like sparks from a flint. Nearer and nearer they came to the river, to the highest point on the bluff. A foam of gold leaves filled the willow trees. Taut as a string stretched over the ridge, the path ran higher and higher. Rosamond's head fell back, till only the treetops glittered in her eyes, which held them like two mirrors. So the sun mounted the morning cloud, and lighted the bluff and then the valley, which opened and showed the river, shining beneath another river of mist, winding and all the colors of flowers.

Then the red horse stood stock-still, and Jamie Lockhart lifted Rosamond down. The wild plum trees were like rolling smoke between him and the river, but he broke the branches and the plums rained down as he carried her under. He stopped and laid her on the ground, where, straight below, the river flowed as slow as sand, and robbed her of that which he had left her the day before.

Now when Rosamond got home from that expedition, the first thing Salome said to her was, "Well, where is the milk?"

Rosamond, whose head was spinning like a spin-

The Robber Bridegroom

dle, and who had not had her breakfast yet, said, "I dare say the red horse drank it up."

Then the stepmother knew everything. "You needn't tell me the story now," she said, "for I could tell it to you," and she licked her lip like a bear after a tasty dish of honey. Then she slapped the girl and dragged her into the house by her heels and propped her by the brooms and buckets and looked her up and down, and thought what she could do to her. And it was too bad the way she treated her the whole day,

"The house must be spotless for the arrival of the stranger," said Salome, "and it's tonight Jamie Lockhart is coming to deliver you from this fiend, though it's late in the day for that. And so it is up to you to wash the floor and polish the row of dishes and candlesticks and put fresh candles in, and sweep the hearth and lay the table and bring the water and clean the fowls and catch the pig and roast him, and get the loaves to baking in the ashes."

But if she thought Rosamond would open her mouth, she was sadly mistaken. The girl never complained a time, but took the beatings and the abusings with the tranquillity of an Indian savage, and cared nothing for how she might look.

"Yes, stepmother," she would say every time, and set to with no more care than if she were only threading a needle.

At dark, Clement rode home from Rodney, and Jamie Lockhart was riding beside him.

Salome was there at the door, in a great fancy gown and heels on her shoes to tilt her up, and with jewelry all over her so that she gave out spangles the way a porcupine gives out quills. So Jamie straightaway got out his presents, and for Salome he had brought a little gold snuffbox, which was just right.

Then at the top of her lungs Salome called Rosamond in from the kitchen, and if she had thought the girl had been making herself beautiful for Jamie Lockhart, she was badly mistaken. For Rosamond was in a sad state to be seen, with ashes all in her hair and soot on either cheek and her poor tongue all but hanging out, and her dress burned to a fringe all around from the coals, and altogether looking like a poor bewitched creature that could only go in circles.

So then Jamie saw Rosamond and they never recognized each other in the world, for the tables were turned; this time he was too clean and she was too dirty. You would think there had never been two lovers on earth with less memory of meeting in the past than Jamie and Rosamond. So he gave her a glance as if she were the peg on the wall where he would hang his hat if he had one, with never a moment's notice of that true worth which he had sampled, and handed her over his gift, which was nothing less than a paper of the pins taken from her own fine dress he had stolen.

Rosamond was so ragged and dirty that she could do no more than stand there in her tracks, and Clement had to speak up for her and say, "Thank you kindly, and the sweet little thing stands in need of pins to be sure, for she has lost them all as I will tell you with the whisky."

But Rosamond only batted her eyes and dropped

her mouth open. As for Jamie, he shone like the sun from cleanliness, youth, wisdom, and satisfaction, and with the dirt and stain gone from his cheeks he was the perfect stranger to the bandit. So if Jamie did not see his kidnaped beauty standing before him, neither did Rosamond see the first sign of her dark lover, and that was that.

Jamie, whose motto was "Take first and ask afterward," had not learned Rosamond's name or where she lived, with her father and seven vengeful brothers, thinking to find out that information on his next ride through the vicinity of the indigo field, doing one thing at a time according to his practice. And besides, it was either love or business that traveled on his mind, never both at once, and this night it was business. For he had not let Clement go that first time without a memorandum of catching him again and finding more. He took a little walk around the room and began counting up to himself what the man's fortune might be, in case he could get hold of it all.

Then Salome told Rosamond to make haste in serving up the dinner, and she did, just as she was, in her rags. With her own hands she spread the abundance on the table and stood by and waited while the others ate and ate, and kept Jamie's glass filled to the top and even spilling over. And in between times she ran around the table and fanned with the peafowl feather fan to keep the flies away—but in a witless manner, so that once or twice she gave Jamie Lockhart a knock on the head. Clement was almost made to think at one time, when she turned a dipper of gravy

49

into Jamie's lap, that this poor daughter of his did not wish to be rescued. And never once did she even say "I beg your pardon" to him.

Every time Clement said, "Why not take your proper seat, daughter, and let the servant wait upon us?" Rosamond would simply back out of sight, and finally the stepmother said, "She is doing this of her own choice, no doubt, to allow you a chance to talk, for it is a delicate matter with her to be rescued from a bandit, it never having happened to her before." And Jamie did not turn a hair, which made the old woman bite her lip.

"Leave us then, wife, since it is time for earnest conversation," said Clement.

Then Clement told Jamie Lockhart all—all, that is, that he knew himself, for the prize bird of the information was not yet in his net. And Jamie, gathering that some bandit had stolen some daughter's clothes on some spot in the forest wilds, thought that he must truly be a success in the world now, for the rest of them were copying him.

"Will you save the poor girl from this brigand, my friend?" asked Clement. "A reward of great price will be yours if you find the fellow and send such a menace to our womanhood out of the world."

"I cannot remain indifferent to such a request," said Jamie. "What is the reward you mention?"

"Deliver my daughter," said Clement, "and she is yours."

Then Jamie gave a start, you may be sure, to think of the poor disgraced creature that had let a pea-

Rosamond, disheveled

fowl feather fan knock his head off, as being his own wife. His eyes looked to the side, like a horse's near the quicksands, and the next moment he jumped up and said, "I must think first, for I am a busy man." And he began walking up and down.

Salome, whose ear had been at the crack, came to take his arm a while, and gave him a raring wink, and spoke a word to him of Rosamond's dreadful pride and conceit and how she needed her lesson, and he did not like the sound of that.

Then Clement took him by the other arm and said that a young thing so sweet and pure as his daughter, who sang the whole day long, and only looked this way for the one night because something had no doubt gone wrong in the kitchen, was more of a reward in herself than his house and lands put together, and Jamie could not say he liked the sound of that either.

Then Rosamond herself came forward, and putting her finger in her mouth like a little long-drawered creature from a covered wagon, said:

"Here I stand all ragged and dirty!
If you don't come kiss me I'll run like a turkey!"

And when he did, she had mustard on her mouth. And that was the last straw.

"Perhaps," said Jamie to himself as he walked up and down, "I should marry her, for she is rich and will be richer and then die, and all things come to him who waits, but that is not my motto. Why the devil could she not have been beautiful, like that little piece of sugar cane I found for myself in the woods? And it is not as if he had a choice of daughters, but the one only." He thought on, and said to himself, "The wife of a successful bandit should be a lady fit to wear fine dresses and jewels, and present an appearance to the world when we go to New Orleans, and make the rest rave with their jealousy. This young creature, however rich, is only a child with a dirty face, and I think the cat has her tongue as well, or the devil her brains."

And besides all that, it is a fact that in his heart Jamie carried nothing less than a dream of true love—something of gossamer and roses, though on this topic he never held conversation with himself, or let the information pass to a soul. And being a man of enterprise in everything, he had collected, whenever it happened to be convenient, numbers of clothes and jewels for this very unknown, that would deck a queen and be missed if a queen left them off. But as for finding this dream on earth, that Jamie was saving until the last, and he had done no work on it as yet except for that very morning; though he hated to waste that.

"What is your answer?" said Clement.

"Well, I will save her, then marry her," said Jamie, "but not now; for I must ride far tonight. I will do it tomorrow."

Clement took his hand and shook it, unable to thank him. Then the stepmother stuck out her wrist to him as if she wanted her hand kissed in the city manner, and when Jamie obliged her, he bowed, and she saw a little bit of berry juice sticking behind his ear. So she guessed everything.

"I wonder what presents he will be bringing next," said she in a loud whisper.

This angered Clement, who said to her, "You will find that men who are generous the way he is generous have needs to match."

Then Jamie waved his hand and rode away alone and still empty-handed, in the confusion of the moonlight, under the twining branches of the trees, bent on no one knew what.

3

Now as soon as jamie had truly dishonored her, Rosamond began to feel a great growing pity for him. And the very next morning after he had come unrecognized to dinner, she set out of the house, carrying a lunch of a small cake she had baked especially, to find where he lived. Up in the window behind her something was looking down—it was either her stepmother or the cat. Rosamond forgot the locust grove, for her path lay another way.

How beautiful it was in the wild woods! Black willow, green willow, cypress, pecan, katalpa, magnolia, persimmon, peach, dogwood, wild plum, wild cherry, pomegranate, palmetto, mimosa, and tulip trees were growing on every side, golden-green in the deep last days of the Summer. Up overhead the cuckoo sang. A quail with her young walked fat as the queen across the tangled path. A flock of cardinals flew up like a fan opening out from the holly bush. The fox looked out from his hole.

On and on she went, deeper and deeper into the forest, and its sound was all around. She heard something behind her, but it was only a woodpecker pecking with his ivory bill. She thought there was a savage there, but it was only a deer which was looking so hard at her. Once she thought she heard a baby crying, but it was a wildcat down in the cane.

At last she crossed a dark ravine and came to a place where two long rows of black cedars were, and at the end sat a house with the door standing open. It was a little house not as pretty as her own, made of cedar logs all neatly put together, and looking and smelling like something good to eat.

So she began walking up the lane, holding the cake in her hands, and when she did she heard a voice saying,

> "Turn back, my bonny,
> Turn away home."

And there was a raven, sitting in a cage which hung at the window.

But she kept on until she got there, and then went up and knocked modestly at the door. However, though her ears were filled with listening, there was no answer to be heard. So she looked through the window and then she looked through the door, but it was all dark and she could see nothing, and so she walked in.

"Is there anybody here?" she called.

But if there was an answer, she couldn't hear it, and so she walked through the house, from the one room to the other. She took a candle she carried in her apron and held it lighted before her. But nobody was there at all, except the raven in the cage, who said once more, when he saw her out of his bright eyes,

> "Turn again, my bonny,
> Turn away home."

"I'll do nothing of the kind," said Rosamond, who had had enough commands from her stepmother.

Everything was in the greatest disorder, bags and saddles lay in the middle of the floor, the remains of big fires lay as if suddenly quenched in the fireplaces. Jugs and long knives, coats and boots of all sizes, tallow candles, and a wonderful bridle of silver and gold were lying in a heap. A young rat sat up like a squirrel at the head of the table, in front of a row of dirty, empty plates. And there in the very middle of the table, close beside a platter with the head of a black bear on it, was Rosamond's own beautiful green silk dress, rolled up into a ball like a bundle of so many quilting pieces.

The first thing she did was to put on her own dress, and then, having nothing else to do, she rearranged all the furniture in the rooms and then washed all the plates and the big knives the robbers had been eating with. Then she hung everything on pegs that she could lift up, and shoveled away the ashes and got down on her knees and scrubbed the hearth until it shone brightly. She carried in the wood and laid a new fire, and was just putting the kettle on to boil when she heard a great clatter in the yard, and the robbers were coming home.

Rosamond hid behind a big barrel in the corner and in they came, with their spotted hounds panting around them. Jamie Lockhart rose up the tallest, his face all covered with the berry juice, just like the day before. He was the leader.

As soon as they saw what had happened to the house, they all stopped as dead as if they had been knocked on the head from behind.

"What grandeur is this?" shouted Jamie in anger.

"What bastard has been robbing the place?" cried the others. "For half the things are missing!"

Then they rushed about turning things over and pulling things down and looking under the tables and stools and between the featherbeds, undoing all of Rosamond's hard work, and at last they found Rosamond sitting behind the barrel, wearing her dress and eating her little cake.

"The first time we went away without a sentry to watch the door, a woman got in!" they said. "Kill her!" they cried.

And they were going to kill her, but she said, "Have some cake."

So each one of them took a piece of cake, and she said she had baked it herself.

The robbers began to argue about what to do with her then, but Jamie, who was their leader and was called nothing but "the Chief," said, "That business can wait till later. First we must count up our booty and divide it, for that is the order of affairs."

So they sat down to count up the worth of this and that, with one who could count keeping close track of it all, and Rosamond had to wait until they had finished.

"Now," said Jamie. "As to the girl, we must either keep her or kill her, for there is nothing midway about any of this."

"Kill her," said one, who was the smallest and who had gotten the smallest piece of cake.

"No, keep her," said the rest, "because she can cook for us and keep the fire up."

"That is settled then," said Jamie, "according to the vote of the band," and having sent them out to stable the horses, he grabbed Rosamond and kissed her as hard as he could, saying if the vote had gone otherwise he would have put the ones who voted wrong out of the way for keeps, since he was running things around there.

So Rosamond stayed and kept house for the robbers. And at first the life was like fairyland. Jamie was only with her in the hours of night, and rode away before the dawn, but he spoke as kind and sweet words as anyone ever could between the hours of sunset and sunrise.

In the daytime, in the silence of noon, while they were all away, she cooked and washed and baked and scrubbed, and sang every song she knew, backwards and forwards, until she was through with them. She washed the robbers' shirts till she wore them out with her washing, and then one evening they brought her home for a surprise a spinning-wheel that had come their way, at great inconvenience, and so she spun and manufactured all they would need for the cold Winter coming. She packed them lunches to take with them in the mornings, a bucket for each, in case they became separated before they would have their food at noon over the fire of an oak tree. And she wove a mat of canes and rushes and made them wipe their feet when they came in at the door.

So the day was hard but the night canceled out the day. When the moon went sailing like a boat through the heavens, between long radiant clouds, all lunar sand bars lying in the stream, and the stars like little fishes nibbled at the night, then it was time for the bandits to ride home. Rosamond waited alone but not afraid. At last they were there, and eating their hot supper, and Jamie came all weary from his riding and robbing, to fling off his sword and his boots and fall on the featherbed, where he would place his head on the softer pillow of her bosom and his face would settle down from all his adventures.

But when she tried to lead him to his bed with a candle, he would knock her down and out of her senses, and drag her there. However, if Jamie was a thief after Rosamond's love, she was his first assistant in the deed, and rejoiced equally in his good success.

She begged him every night to wash off the stains from his face so that she could see just once what he really looked like, and she swore that she believed he would be handsome, but he would never do it. He told her that this was for the best of reasons, and she

Rosamond at the spinning wheel

had to be content with that. Sometimes she would wake up out of her first sleep and study his sleeping face, but she did not know the language it was written in. And she would look out the window and see a cloud put up a mask over the secret face of the moon, and she would hear the pitiful cries of the night creatures. Then it was enough to make her afraid, as if the whole world were circled by a band of Indian savages, and she would shake poor Jamie until he shouted up out of his sleep, and rouse him up to see his eyes come open. She would often wipe the rain away from his face when he came home, but nothing, it seemed, could penetrate those stains. No matter how she scrubbed, until he would let out a yell, the stains were just as dark as before. And sometimes, because he had told her that he had bound himself to an heiress, she was afraid he might get up and fly away through the window while she was fast asleep; so she would not let him go until up the gentle levee of the morning clouds the sun would climb to touch the brim, and the bandits flew over the ridge.

The only thing that divided his life from hers was the raiding and the robbing that he did, but that was like his other life, that she could not see, and so she contented herself with loving all that was visible and present of him as much as she was able.

The trees were golden under the sky. The grass was as soft as a dream and the wind blew like the long rising and falling breath of Summer when she has just fallen asleep. One day Jamie did not ride away with the others, and then the day was night and the woods were the roof over their heads. The tender flames of the myrtle trees and the green smoke of the cedars were the fires of their hearth. In the radiant noon they found the shade, and ate the grapes from the muscadine vines. The spice-dreams rising from the fallen brown pine needles floated through their heads when they stretched their limbs and slept in the woods. The stream lay still in the golden ravine, the water glowing darkly, the colors of fruits and nuts.

"Remember your own words," said the bandits to Jamie, as they were riding away without him to a rendezvous. "'Who followeth not up his own work will fail.'"

"I cannot fail," said Jamie, and he half pulled out his little dirk.

For he thought he had it all divisioned off into time and place, and that many things were for later and for further away, and that now the world had just begun.

"All these treasures are for you," he said to Rosamond at night when the bounty was counted out.

"Thank you," she replied, and sorted and stored it all—even labeled it, with the date if she could keep account of it in the dream of time passing. And though she did not know when she would ever find use for a thousand pieces of English silver or the scalp of a Creek, she took tender care of each item.

And every night Jamie would come in with a mess of quail, bobolinks, purple finches, or bluebirds, which he would heap on the table and tell her to dress. Once he brought a heron, the color of Venetian glass, and it tasted as wild as a wild pear, but there was not enough of heron breast for any to eat except Jamie and Rosamond, and the rest ate buffalo meat in silence, under the smoke of the torches.

If her dead mother could have seen Rosamond then, she would never have troubled herself to come back one more time from the repose of Heaven to console and protect her, and could have fully given herself over to the joys of Paradise from then on; that is, if she could overlook from that place the fact that Jamie was a bandit; for Rosamond had quite forgotten the locket.

The only thing that could possibly keep her from being totally happy was that she had never seen her lover's face. But then the heart cannot live without something to sorrow and be curious over.

Now on the day that he had followed Rosamond to the robbers' house, all had gone well with Goat, and he was right at her heels, if she had turned around she would have been behind him, until she knocked at the robbers' door.

At first there had been no answer at all, and Goat decided they must have come on the wrong day. But then the raven had looked at them and said,

> "Turn back, my bonny,
> Turn away home."

So Goat, who never disobeyed any orders as plain as that, had turned at once and gone back to his mother.

"Hello, Mother, I'm home again," said he, butting

his way in to the kitchen. "A raven advised me to get back at once: what's the news?"

"Oh, cark and care," said his mother. "Did you bring back any money?"

"No," said he, "but I expect to receive some at any moment, for the lady I work for is very rich."

"Then it's a good thing," said his mother, "or I would be wishing I had strangled you at birth for all the comfort I get out of you."

"Are my six sisters married off yet?" asked Goat.

"They are just as they were yesterday, and that is unwed," said the mother.

"You have only to wait until I am paid for my work," said Goat, "and they will come rushing at all six of them as if they were in burning houses."

Then he told her good-by and set off up the hill to ask Salome for his pay.

"What, are you back so soon?" said Salome, when they had hidden in the orchard.

So he said he was back and that it was soon.

"Did you follow her this time?" Salome asked.

So he said yes, he followed her; that is, until a raven spoke up and told him it was time to go home.

"What raven?" cried Salome, for she did not know what raven he could mean.

Well, he said, it was simply the raven they kept to answer the door, he supposed, when they were not at home. And now might he have his pay?

"Go break your neck!" cried Salome. "Your mother should have strangled you in your cradle."

Goat said that made two that thought so, but that

was not many. And he asked what if he came back to see her tomorrow, would she pay him then?

"Oh," said Salome, "when are you going to take your brains out and put them back in straight? Go to this house again, discount anything said to you by a raven, and when you find where Rosamond has gone, see what she does, and whether she cries or not, and come back and tell me."

"And when you have heard, will you pay me then?" asked Goat.

"Now you have it in your head," said Salome. "And get gone!"

Then she boxed both his ears and he set out, first passing through the chicken yard and letting a hen out of the coop, and then through the pigsty, where he let out a little pig with red spots. On second thought, he put both of these and a big red peach into his bag as advance payment to provide against starvation.

He was going along and going along through the deep woods, and went part of the way with a little wild boar that trotted as proudly as a horse, and had almost reached the robbers' house when he saw another place. There, up an avenue of cedar trees, at the entrance of a cave built of rock, sitting by a fire, was a bandit named the Little Harp, and he was just as ugly as it was possible to be. But Goat did not mind that, and sang out, "Good morning, mister! What are you up to? How are you feeling and how is everything with you? Is there anything that I could do for you? And how far is it from here to where the kidnaped young lady goes and raps on the door?"

Little Harp blinked his eyes and smiled, for nothing pleased him on a fine day like a lack of brains.

"Come here," said he, "and stay with me. I will give you work to do."

"Gladly," replied Goat, "but I am already working for another, a very rich lady, an old stepmother, who wants me to see that her stepdaughter is well kidnaped by a bandit. But I don't see why a young fellow like me could not take care of two commissions at one time."

"That is the way to talk," said the Little Harp. "You will come up in the world."

"How much are you going to pay me every month?" asked Goat, taking a seat on a rock and stretching his legs.

"Never mind," said the Little Harp. "Just do whatever I tell you, and you won't regret it."

"What will you want first," asked Goat, "if I do work for you?"

"Well," said Little Harp, "I might take a notion for a big fat hen."

"If that is all, I don't think that will be very hard," said Goat, and reaching into his little bag he pulled out the hen, which indeed the Little Harp had been watching with watering mouth from the first moment, if he had not smelled it down the way. So the Little Harp took it. "I must consider," said he. He wrung the hen by the neck, plucked a feather off it, passed it through his little fire, and swallowed it down. "Yes, I believe you could do the work," he said. "You are hired. But now there is one thing that you must remember never to do, as long as you work for me. Never open the little trunk you will see standing by my featherbed inside the cave."

"If I do, you may cut off my ears," promised Goat.

"You may hear something say, 'Let me out,'" said Little Harp, "but you must answer, 'Not yet!' If you open the trunk even one inch, that will be the end of you."

"And will the money stop then too?" asked Goat.

"Completely," said Little Harp. "There is not a chance in the world of your ever getting another cent once you are dead."

"I agree to the terms," said Goat, and they shook hands.

"Now," said Goat, "what would you like me to do?"

"Well," said Little Harp, "I feel a fancy coming over me for a pig with red spots, but if that is impossible to find, don't look for it."

"Impossible my foot," said Goat. "I can get it for you as easy as breathing," and he pulled out his pig.

"Go pickle him," said Little Harp.

"Would you not rather have a peach?" asked Goat. "For that won't take as long."

"Yes," said the Little Harp, "I believe I would rather have a peach."

So he ate the peach on the spot, seed, fuzz, and all, and Goat asked him with the last swallow, "What next?"

"Next I would like a girl, kidnaped and brought to my door here," said Little Harp. "But I dare say you will not know where to find one."

"I have no kidnaped girl with me," said Goat, "but I have one in my mind. How soon do you want her?"

"By tomorrow," said Little Harp.

"It's as good as over with," said Goat. "You may imagine her now, skipping over the hill."

"Let me see her little finger first," said Little Harp. "Then, if I like that much, I will take her."

Goat was so overjoyed that he got up and did a little dance called "Rabbit Hash." Then away he went.

Little Harp went inside his cave and stretched his feet on the featherbed to wait.

Then there was a voice which had the sound of coming out of a little trunk, and it said, "Let me out!"

"Not yet!" cried Little Harp, and he began to cry, "Oh, you do plague me so, to be nothing more than a head wrapped up in blue mud, though I know your eyes and your tongue do stick out as red as fire, the way you came down off the pole in Rodney Square." And he said, "Oh, Big Harp, my brother, please stay in the trunk like a good head, and don't be after me eternally for raiding and murdering, for you give me no rest."

But the voice said, "Let me out!" all the while, even after the Little Harp fell asleep and went to snoring.

Back home in the gully, in came Goat, butting his way through the front door, which was locked, and they were all sitting around the table.

Little Harp

"Good news!" he cried, snatching up a johnnycake. "Sisters, the time for one of you has come. Arise and prepare yourself, for the time is set for tomorrow."

"The time for what?" they said.

"You must listen more closely, if you want to hear wonders," said Goat. "Sisters, all six of you point up your ears, and take this in with the full set of twelve. I am now working on the side for a gentleman up yonder in a cave, and when I said, 'What do you want?' he said first a hen, then a pig, then a peach, and before long he was dead for a wife. And although I do not speak all that runs to the end of my tongue, I conversed with myself behind my hand, and said, 'Here I am with six hopping virgin sisters in my own family, and my own house a nest of women—this job was designed for me in Heaven!' And I rushed here at once with the good news."

"Well," said the mother, "is he rich?" For she did all the talking for the six daughters.

"Oh, I am sure he must be rich," answered Goat, "for he has, for one thing, a trunk so precious that he talks to it, and lets no one open it even to the extent of an inch."

So all the daughters there in a row began to sit up and toss their hair about.

"Is he handsome?" said the youngest.

"Well," said Goat, "I would not say outright that the gentleman is stamped with beauty, for when I saw him, his head was no larger than something off the orange tree, his forehead was full of bumps like an alligator's, and two teeth stuck out of his mouth like the broadhorns on a flatboat. He came out walking like a goose and dressed like a wild Indian. But beauty is no deeper than the outside, and besides, all six of you are as weighted down with freckles as a fig tree is with figs, which should render you modest."

"Which of us shall marry him?" they asked one another, and fell to giggling.

"Let us send him up the eldest," said the mother, "for she has waited the longest," and so that was decided.

"Be ready at sunup for the kidnaping," said Goat, "and be sure one of your little fingers is as sweet as a rose, or nothing will be doing."

At the same time, Clement and Salome were riding in the little cart over the plantation, which by now had all been harvested.

"Next year," said Salome, and she shaded her eagle eye with her eagle claw, and scanned the lands from east to west, "we must cut down more of the forest, and stretch away the fields until we grow twice as much of everything. Twice as much indigo, twice as much cotton, twice as much tobacco. For the land is there for the taking, and I say, if it can be taken, take it."

"To encompass so much as that is greedy," said Clement. "It would take too much of time and the heart's energy."

"All the same, you must add it on," said Salome. "If we have this much, we can have more." And she petted the little nut-shaped head of the peacock on her lap.

"Are you not satisfied already?" asked her husband.

"Satisfied!" cried Salome. "Never, until we have got rid of this house which is little better than a Kentuckian's cabin, with its puncheon floor, and can live in a mansion at least five stories high, with an observatory of the river on top of that, with twenty-two Corinthian columns to hold up the roof."

"My poor wife, you are ahead of yourself," said Clement, and he felt of her forehead to see if it were hot. And indeed it was burning like fire, for Salome worked her brain day and night to think up her wishes.

"I am doing well enough," said Salome. "It is you whose hand is cold."

"Then it is cold with grief," said Clement.

"Oh, now that that lazy, extravagant daughter of yours is no longer here," said Salome, "we shall be able to count much more on our plans, for now you have no one to will the money to, and so we may as well spend it at once."

"Hold your tongue, wife!" cried Clement, and he raised up and almost put his hands upon her, but he could not, for the poor contamination of her heart broke out through her words until it showed even on her skin, like the signs of the pox, and he could not punish her.

Then Salome, having Clement in her power, sent him out to make fresh application to the Governor for more acres, and resigned to that, he rode away to Rodney.

And there, staying once more at the inn where the landlord with the trembling ears kept hospitality for the travelers, Clement chanced to see Jamie Lockhart again, dressed as fine as anyone out of New Orleans in his button-sewn coat with the sleeves knotted around him capewise.

Now the truth is, Jamie had neglected poor Clement entirely, being so taken up with his daughter, and had never ridden back to do the thing he had promised, but only put it off. So he ran forward now to clasp his hand, and sat him down in the grogshop and bought him a glass of the best Kentucky whisky. Then he told him, as his excuse, that his business had carried him all of a sudden to New Orleans on the very night when he saw him last, where he had been from then till now, as busy as he had ever been in his life, and that he had therefore been unable to ride after the bandit who had frightened his daughter.

"However," said Jamie, "drink down bravely, for it is my belief that the fellow will do her no more harm if he did not do it at first thoughts."

"Alas," said Clement, "while you were gone, he thought of it, for my child is stolen away."

Then the salt tears ran down his cheeks, and Jamie's heart was reached by the old man's sorrow, and after buying him another glass of whisky he spent the night in the same bed again without stealing a cent from him. Indeed, since he had not stolen it yet, he doubted if he ever would, for the old man had trusted the evil world and was the kind of man it would break your heart to rob.

"I have just succeeded in enlarging my plantation twice over," said Clement, when they met again in the morning, "though the size of anything whatever has nothing to do with the peace of mind. My wife will build a tower to overlook the boundaries of her land, while I ride its woods and know it to be a maze without end, for my love is lost in it."

So, in his soft feeling, Jamie declared before he knew it that he would track down this beast if it was the last thing he did, blow his brains out, and marry the poor daughter in the bargain.

For never once, due to the seven rampant brothers which his own kidnaped bride brought into the conversation now and again (whenever he recalled that he was promised to another), did the thought alight on Jamie's head that she might be for one moment the same as Clement's thumb-sucking child. It was the habit of the times for heiresses to disappear, as though swallowed up, and one more or less did not cause Jamie to stop and take notice.

"Tonight," said Jamie now, rising to his feet, "I will ride the woods to the north of here, and you must ride them to the south, and if the man has been running ahead of you, we will head him off."

Clement shook his hand, and when he could speak, it was to say once more, "Save her, and she is yours still."

On the plantation, Clement, inspired by Jamie to the hope of making a rescue that very night, ate a whole roast pig for supper and set out on horseback just as the stars began to come out.

He rode south on the Old Natchez Trace and then took another trail branching off to the deepest woods, a part he had never searched before. The wind shook the long beards of the moss. The lone owls hooted one by one and flew by his head as big as barrels. Near-by in the cane the wildcats frolicked and played, and on he rode, through the five-mile smell of a bear, and on till he came all at once to the bluff where deep down, under the stars, the dark brown wave of the Mississippi was rolling by. That was the place where he had found the river and married Salome. And if he had but known it, that was the place where Jamie Lockhart had carried his daughter, there under the meeting trees at the edge.

Clement's horse stopped, and all of a sudden there was a rustle of the leaves and a ghost or a shape went by behind him. In the next moment Clement was riding in pursuit, for he thought it was the bandit now for sure, and he rode and rode furiously, though it seemed to him that he had lost the way and that he was only charging in a circle; and this had happened to him before. But then he heard the same sound, and he brought his horse to a stop and jumped off his back. And although up until that moment he had thought all he defended too sacred for the privilege of violence, he now flung himself forward with such force that the wind left his body for a moment. He ran headlong

The deep woods

through the dark, and then it seemed he clasped the very sound itself in his arms. He could feel the rude powerful grip of a giant or a spirit, and once he was brushed by a feather such as the savages wore, and they threshed about and beat down the earth for a long time. It was as dark as it could possibly be, for the stars seemed to have gone in and left the naked night overhead, and so Clement wrestled with his monster without any aid from the world at all. He tossed it to the ground and it flew up again, he bent it back with all his strength and it would not yield, it fought with the arms of a whirlwind and flung him on the ground, and he was about to give up, but then it clung to him like the Old Man of the Sea and he could not get out from under. At last with a great crash he threw himself upon it and it went down, and he sat there holding it down where it lay with his own body for the rest of the night, not daring to close his eyes for his concern, and for thinking he had won over wickedness. And it was not till the eye of the red sun looked over the ridge that Clement saw he had fought all night with a willow tree.

In the meanwhile, Jamie was riding the woods to the north and wishing he were home instead. He had just started to stain his face with the berry juice when he heard all of a sudden the sounds of screaming come out of a cave in the hillside.

"There, I have found the witless thing, without even trying," he said; "for it would be like her to scream at her bandit the whole night through and give him no peace, out of pure perversity." And he rode straight up to the door of the cave and threw a rock against it.

"One at a time!" came a voice from the inside. "If you're the next sister, you must wait till tomorrow!"

And "Oh! Oh! Oh!" came the screaming.

"Open up," cried Jamie. "If you're after doing a murder, I can give you aid."

"Can you now?" asked the Little Harp, for of course it was he inside with one of Goat's six sisters, and he came to the door and peeped through the chink.

"Here, you see, is the very rope to tie her up with," said Jamie, holding up nothing in the dark.

Then the Little Harp let him in, and Jamie followed him back in the cave to where he had one of Goat's sisters standing straight up in the middle of the floor with her apron tied over her head.

"Well, proud, dirty thing," said Jamie to her, for he had no doubt it was Clement's dim-witted daughter, and he gave her a mock kiss, "what are you doing inside there?"

"Oh! Oh! Oh!" she screamed back.

"She does nothing but scream," said the Little Harp. "That is her gift, and I would just as soon try to sleep in the room with a hyena."

"Why did you tie her up so snug?" asked Jamie. "You let the more dangerous hands and feet go free and only confine the harmless head."

"Oh, I have her blindfolded because she is so ugly," said the Little Harp. "I had her kidnaped sight unseen and test untested, you see, being given to understand she was in demand by another bandit, and never knowing that this was the masterpiece I would get. But as soon as I saw her little finger, I told her to go drown herself in the river."

"Oh!" screamed this sister of Goat's.

"But when I told her that," continued the Little Harp, "she told me that she was only one of six thriving sisters, all as strong as oxen, and that the whole company of them would come up here after me and beat my head to a pulp if I did not untie her."

"Ah yes, the brand of that speech is familiar to me," said Jamie, and he only laughed at the poor creature's fury, and gave her another peck that she did not know was coming.

"If you were to take your rope and tie the remainder of her up," said Little Harp, "do you suppose that would make her hush, or put her out of order for a little while?"

"That is a brilliant solution you have got there," said Jamie, thinking to have some fun with the two sillies, since the night was wasted anyway, and so he drew his hands around the girl's middle and gave her a little squeeze. But if she had screamed loudly enough before to be heard in church at Rodney, she screamed loudly enough next to be heard down at Fort Rosalie.

"That was wrong," said the Little Harp. "I would give anything for you not to have done that."

"There, we have got her started going louder instead of softer," said Jamie, "and I fear there will be no stopping her now. She will go on in this direction, getting louder and louder, until the rocks of this cave will come falling in, and bury us all alive. Why, my friend, don't you marry her instead?"

"Though it would keep me from deafness and a landslide, I would not do it," said the Little Harp, shaking his tiny head.

"Well, then," said Jamie, looking about, and thinking on the side that a bandit, however slow-witted, who could not do better than this cave must have something amiss somewhere. "How about putting the maiden in the trunk?"

"No! No! No! Never!" cried the Little Harp, and he ran and held the lid down. "For oh, the noise leaks out of the trunk too!" And he put his ear to the lock. "Listen!" he said.

But Jamie heard nothing at all, and at this show of silliness he thought it was time to change his tune. So he went to snatch up the girl without further dilly-dallying and take her home to Clement.

But the Little Harp came waddling forward like an old goose, and there held up in his right hand was the carving knife.

"I won't marry her," said he. "So come let's kill her! I'll hold her down, and you slice her down the center."

At this the poor girl nearly lost her voice, but she recovered it in time to scream a flock of bats down from the ceiling before she toppled over like the dead at their touch.

Jamie jumped with all his might on the Little Harp and dragged him in the corner.

"The game is over," said Jamie, "and the joke is

Goat's oldest sister

told. You are not the fool I took you to be, but another fool entirely, and I ought to break all your bones where you need them most. Now tell me your name and I will tell you to get out of the country."

"My name is Little Harp, and my brother's name is Big Harp, but they cut off his head in Rodney and stuck it on a pole."

"Then get out of the country," said Jamie, "for I have heard of the Harps, that ran about leaving dead bodies over the countryside as thick as flies on the dumpling."

"Aha, but I know who you are too," said Little Harp, sticking out his tongue in a point, and his little eyes shining. "Your name is Jamie Lockhart and you are the bandit in the woods, for you have your two faces on together and I see you both."

At that, Jamie staggered back indeed, for he allowed no one who had seen him as a gentleman to see him as a robber, and no one who knew him as a robber to see him without the dark-stained face, even his bride.

He half pulled out his little dirk to kill the Little Harp then and there. But his little dirk, not unstained with blood, held back and would not touch the feeble creature. Something seemed to speak to Jamie that said, "This is to be your burden, and so you might as well take it." So he put the little dirk back and contented himself with one more blow with his arm, to knock the Little Harp's wind out for an hour or so.

Then he picked up the girl and set her up on his horse, still dead in her faint and sitting up as nice and

79

stiff as a bird that is looked at by a snake, and so without bothering to unwrap her, Jamie took her off to Clement's house.

By now it was daylight, and he stopped and took the stain off the one side of his face and tied his coat about him, and then he knocked at the door.

"Here is your daughter," he said to Clement, and the old man nearly died with joy, but then he saw the foot sticking out and then the rough red hand. "My daughter has skin as white as a lily," he said, "and her foot is small.

"Oh, God in Heaven," he said, and then the apron fell off of its own accord and he saw the poor fish face looking at him. "Jamie Lockhart, you have rescued the wrong daughter. This is none of mine."

Then there was general misery, except for Goat's sister, who was rather pleased than sorry, now that the whole thing was over and she was not lying at the bottom of the river, and she went off home to tell the rest of her sisters the horrible things that had happened to her.

"But the worst of all," said Jamie to himself, as he stopped in the black ravine and stained his face again, "is that I have let the Little Harp go." He wondered now why he had done it, and he said, "This is going to be a burden to me," for he knew that by the time he got home, the Little Harp would have moved in.

4

THE NEXT MORNING, AFTER THE DOUBLE FAILURE to rescue his daughter from the bandit in the woods, Clement was sitting with his wife on his little veranda. All at once the front gate opened with a little sound, and there came Rosamond up the path.

They could hardly believe their eyes, until she had come and given them a kiss apiece.

"Well, where is your husband?" asked the step-mother.

"He sent his respects to my parents," said Rosamond, "but he is too busy to come himself."

Salome looked first at Rosamond's belt and then at her countenance, and was mortified to see no signs of humility in either place.

"Haughty and proud as ever, I see," she remarked, getting up to pace about her in a circle, "though the whole world knows you are no better than that gully girl who ran to the cave of the Little Harp and got blinders tied on her head for her trouble."

But Rosamond took out the presents she had brought back to them, very fine and expensive articles indeed, speaking well for her prosperity, and handed them out.

As for Clement, he embraced his daughter time after time, and was so filled with the joy of seeing her that he could not think up a single question to ask her.

So Salome said, "I dare say your robber-bridegroom has got enough of you and sent you packing."

"No, stepmother," said Rosamond, "for he will not let me leave his side."

"Then he keeps you a prisoner, does he?" cried Salome. "Just as I thought!"

"No, stepmother," said Rosamond, "for I stay of my own accord. But I thought of my father to whom I had not said good-by and it was more than I could bear, and I began to beg and to beg until at last this very morning I received permission to come here. But it is for a short time only."

"I dare say when you return you will find that your bird has flown," said the stepmother next, for she pretended to know a great deal about the way of bandits.

"No, stepmother. We have a trust in one another that this separation cannot break," said Rosamond, but her stepmother only began to smile and ponder, and ponder and smile.

"Tell me, my ladybird," said Clement when he could speak through his delight and see through his tears, "are you happy?"

"Yes, Father," said Rosamond. "Although my husband is a bandit, he is a very good one."

"And does he bring you home fine clothes, dozens of beautiful dresses and petticoats too?" asked Salome, and Rosamond knew what she meant, but still she said, "Yes, indeed."

Then Clement thought, "She has met the man who can keep her from lying, and she is entirely out of the habit." And he was puzzled, and thought, "I should like to meet this strict bandit who has taught my daughter to be truthful."

"Where is your home, my child?" he asked.

"It is not far from here," said Rosamond, "but it might as well be a hundred miles, for it is so deep and dark in the woods, that no one knows the way out except my husband, who brought me."

Now the stepmother drew closer in upon Rosamond as she paced her circle, and said, "Does your husband kill the travelers where they stand, when he has finished with them, and leave them there in their blood, like all the rest?"

"I believe not," replied Rosamond, "but that I could not say, for he has never told me and I never asked him."

"What? You poor ignorant girl!" cried the stepmother. "I suppose you will say next that you do not even know his name for he has never told you!"

"That is correct," replied Rosamond.

"What!" cried the stepmother, and she was drawing in closer still. "You have been kept in darkness! Now do not tell me you have never seen the man by the light of day without his robber's disguise."

For although Goat had failed every time to make

his report to Salome, she had divined these things for herself by means of the very wickedness in her heart.

"That is correct too," said Rosamond, and how her stepmother laughed to hear it, like a jay bird in the tree.

"Now tell us," said she finally, and she stood just above Rosamond's head looking down upon her, "whether or not you are truly married, in the eyes of heaven and the church."

So Rosamond looked back and forth between her father and her stepmother, and then, "Oh indeed," she said. "Father Danny O'Connell married us."

"God help him then," cried Clement, jumping to his feet, "for I see him on every journey I make to Rodney, and he has never told me."

"Ah, then, that is because the good father was drunk the day he married us," said Rosamond.

"Well, then, if he married you in the church, how is it you were not seen by the whole population of Rodney when you came down the steps?" said Salome.

"Oh, he did not marry us in the church," said Rosamond, "but at home in the woods."

"How did he know where to go, if I could not find it?" asked Clement, with his sorrow on his heart.

"That is because he did not go of his own knowledge or control," said Rosamond. "For my husband kidnaped him and brought him there. My husband rode down the streets of Rodney, and there was the priest, and he reached right down and got him like a hawk, and took him home. He was just a little drunk to begin with, so my husband set him up on his own horse, nicely sideways because of the cloth, and rode him home, and there on the hearth he married us, as drunk as a lord at the time, but very binding in the way he put it."

"How did poor Father O'Connell ever get so bad as that?" asked Clement. "For all that he is a good shot, a horse judge, and a sampler of Madeira, I have never seen Father O'Connell so beside himself he did not know which sinner he was giving an almo to on the streets."

"It was my husband that got him so drunk," said Rosamond. "First when they came, they had a little bragging contest, each surpassing the other until nobody won, and then my husband started a little contest to see who could empty the most from a jug for the count of ten, and all the rest stood around in a ring and they counted up to twenty-five. It was because of his sporting blood that Father O'Connell could not set down the jug, and he won."

"These competitions are dangerous things," said Clement. "I myself would have been the loser of more than my sense and my money once, if it had not been for Jamie Lockhart."

"And did the priest marry you then?" Salome asked, and she bent down over Rosamond and looked ready to gobble her up.

But Rosamond said, "Yes, then Father O'Connell said the marriage for my husband and me, and the whole house was decorated with flowers in gold vases," and her voice was as clear as a bell.

"It is strange that he remembers nothing of this,"

said Clement to himself. "He must have thought he had been only to fairyland, with all the glitter about, and never mentioned it."

There has to be a first time for everything, and at that moment the stepmother gave Rosamond a look of true friendship, as if Rosamond too had got her man by unholy means. But Rosamond began to wilt then, like a flower cut and left in the sun.

So the next day Salome got Rosamond away alone and they were sitting by the well, like a blood mother and daughter.

"My child," said the stepmother, "do I understand that you have never seen your husband's face?"

"Never," said Rosamond. "But I am sure he must be very handsome, for he is so strong."

"That signifies nothing," said the stepmother, "and works neither way. I fear, my dear, that you feel in your bosom a passion for a low and scandalous being, a beast who would like to let you wait on him and serve him, but will not do you the common courtesy of letting you see his face. It can only be for the reason that he is some kind of monster."

And she talked on until she saw the pride and triumph fading from Rosamond with every breath she took. For Rosamond did not think the trickery went so deep in her stepmother that it did not come to an end, but made her solid like an image of stone in the garden; and her time had come to believe her.

So Salome drew so close to Rosamond that they could look down the well and see one shadow, and she whispered in her ear, "There is one way to find out what your husband looks like, and if you want me to tell you: ask me."

"What way is that?" asked Rosamond, for at last she had to know.

"It is a little recipe, my dear, for removing berry stains," said Salome, "and there are no berry stains in the world so obstinate that this brew will not rub them out."

"What brew is that?" asked Rosamond, for she had to learn.

"Pay close attention, and stamp it on your brain," said the stepmother, "so you can remember it until you get home."

Then she repeated the recipe for removing berry stains from the face, as follows: Take three fresh eggs and break them into clear rain water. Stir until this is mixed, then boil it on the stove. Take the curd and set it off to cool. Add a little saffron, a little rue, and a little pepper. Throw into a quart of drinking-whisky and churn it up and down until it foams. Sponge it on, and the stains will go away.

"Remember that," said Salome. "It can't fail."

And then she reached down and pulled Rosamond's own mother's locket out of her little pouch and dangled it up before the girl.

"You forgot this, in your haste to leave," she said. "And you had better take it this time, for you might need it." Then she put it around Rosamond's neck and fastened it with her own hands.

She advised her to take one of the tomahawks with her also, to protect herself with, in case her husband should turn out to be too horrible to look at; but Rosamond was not that far gone that she would take it.

Then the girl thanked her for all her trouble and advice, and embraced her around the neck, and kissed her father, and said she intended to go back to her husband at once, sooner than she was expected, so as to surprise him.

"How happy he will be," said Clement. "And poor Jamie Lockhart!"

"Or how unhappy he will be, one or the other," said Salome, and then she ran in at the last moment to write the recipe for removing berry juice stains down on paper with her fine black quill, in case Rosamond might not remember everything that went into it.

While she was out of the way, it was Clement's time to speak to Rosamond alone, and he asked her about her husband for the last time.

"If being a bandit were his breadth and scope, I should find him and kill him for sure," said he. "But since in addition he loves my daughter, he must be not the one man, but two, and I should be afraid of killing the second. For all things are double, and this should keep us from taking liberties with the outside world, and acting too quickly to finish things off. All things are divided in half—night and day, the soul and body, and sorrow and joy and youth and age, and sometimes I wonder if even my own wife has not been the one person all the time, and I loved her beauty so well at the beginning that it is only now that the ugli-

The Locket and the Recipe

ness has struck through to beset me like a madness. And perhaps after the riding and robbing and burning and assault is over with this man you love, he will step out of it all like a beastly skin, and surprise you with his gentleness. For this reason, I will wait and see, but it breaks my heart not to have seen with my own eyes what door you are walking into and what your life has turned out to be."

Then Salome came running with the recipe written out and folded. "Hold this in your hand," she said.

So Rosamond took it and set out.

"Shall I walk part of the way with you?" her father called, but she went on alone, into the woods.

This time, Rosamond was afraid as she ran along, and she stumbled over the stones and was caught by the sharp thorns. She turned and looked behind her all the way, as if she were frightened of being followed by a beast which would tear her apart. A little whirlwind blew over the grass and pulled her hair down and tangled it with twigs. The little ravine was cold and gray, the mist lay on it, and the stream ran choked with yellow weeds, and the squirrels were shrieking through the woods.

At last she came to the lane between the two rows of cedars with the little house there at the end, and the door standing open and dark as before, but now scattered with fallen leaves. So she began walking up the lane, holding the little recipe in her hand and wearing the locket around her neck, and she said, "If my mother could see me now, her heart would break."

But when she said that, a cloud rolled over the sky and a cold wind sprang up like Winter-time, and just as she came to the house the yellow lightning gave a flash like swords dueling over the rooftop. There at the window hung the raven in the cage, which had gone all rusty, and Rosamond had forgotten all about him. So he said,

"Turn back, my bonny,
Turn away home."

But in she went.

There in the dark hall she stood and looked through the door. All the bandits were there except her husband, and there was a strange bandit in his place, standing in the middle of the room while they lay on the floor and laughed at him. He was the ugliest man she had ever seen in her life, and she thought her heart would stop beating and her breath would stop in her throat before she could hide down behind the barrel, safe out of sight.

The whisky and the wine were going round, and the bandits were all as dirty and filthy as if she had left them for a year instead of a day. The whole house was tumbled and wrecked, with everything topsy-turvy and the rats back inside and running about unharmed. All her hard work had gone for nothing, and it was as if she had never done it.

The strange bandit was the Little Harp, who had moved in to live with Jamie Lockhart, not failing to bring his little trunk, which was there beside him.

And all the men were lying about him and listening to him as if he were their chief, and nobody spoke of their real chief, or asked where he could be.

The jug went round from hand to hand, and soon all the robbers were drunk and the Little Harp was the the drunkest of all.

"Where is the girl that you have here?" he cried. "Where do you keep her? Bring her in and give her to me!"

And then all the robbers laughed in great good spirits at the way the Little Harp asked for the girl that belonged to the king of the bandits, which was a thing they had often wished they could do themselves.

"She is away on a visit," they told the Little Harp, "and besides, she belongs to our chief."

"But your chief belongs to me!" cried the Little Harp. "He is bound over to me body and soul, because I saw what I saw and know what I know, and for that I may have his woman and all."

Then he set up such a din to have her that one of the robbers went out and brought in another young girl, but with long black hair, and pushed her through the circle into the Little Harp's arms.

"There she is!" they said to quiet him. And for a joke, it was an Indian girl.

He asked them first if they would swear she was not out of the gully but the true bride of the bandit king, and they all swore so long and so hard that Rosamond herself was almost ready to believe that she stood out in the room under the robbers' eyes and was not hiding down behind the barrel.

So the Little Harp said, "What will I do with her first? Bring her the Black Drink!"

The Black Drink was an Indian drink, and some people called it the Sleepy Drink, because whoever tasted it fell over like a dead man with his eyes rolled back, and could not be roused by anything in the world for three days.

So the girl fought and screamed, but they held the Black Drink to her lips and made her drink it and she fell over like the dead, with her hair and her arms swinging in front of her.

All the roomful laughed to see her, and the Little Harp took out his sharp knife and said, "Next I will cut off her little finger, for it offends me," and he cut off her wedding finger, and it jumped in the air and rolled across the floor into Rosamond's lap. But though she thought she would die of fright, Rosamond stayed where she was, as still as a mouse, and none of them saw where the finger went or hunted for it, for it had no ring on it.

"And now I will teach her the end of her life, for that is the thing she comes here lacking," said the Little Harp, and he threw the girl across the long table, among the plates and all, where the remains of all the meals lay where they were left, with the knives and forks sticking in them, and flung himself upon her before their eyes.

"You have killed her now," they said, and it was true: she was dead.

But just at that moment there was the sound of

The Indian girl's hand

horse's hoofs, and next a terrible shout at the door, and Jamie Lockhart came in.

"What has he done?" he asked, and pointed to the Little Harp where he stood bragging among them all.

"I have killed your bride, and that is the first payment," said the Little Harp, holding up the sharp knife. "And the next thing, I will speak out your name and cast evil upon it."

"No, you will not!" shouted Jamie, and for the second time he leaped upon the Little Harp and with his two hands choked the wind out of him for a while.

"Take him away," he told the others, "for I will not have him sleeping with me. Roll him down the hill and let him lie, though if the wolves don't touch him, he'll be back with me tomorrow."

So the other bandits carried the Little Harp out and pitched him over the bushes, for Jamie still would not put an end to him: something would not let him have that satisfaction yet.

"Now what has he done?" Jamie cried, and he ran to the dead girl stretched on the table, but when he lifted up her hair it was black, and he saw it was the wrong girl. Then he could not speak at all, but fell upon his bed.

Then Rosamond came out from behind the barrel, and touched him where he lay, and told him she had returned, to lie by his side.

But when she woke up out of her first sleep, she looked at him dreaming there with his face stained dark with the berry juice, and she was torn as she had never been before with an anguish to know his name and his true appearance. For the coming of death and danger had only driven her into her own heart, and it was no matter what he had told her, she could wait no longer to learn the identity of her true love.

Up she got and away she crept, and made up the brew which would wipe away the stains. Then she crept back with some of it on a bit of rag. She took Jamie's head on her lap while he still slept and dreamed, and held up the lighted candle to see by, and set to her task. Lo and behold, the brew worked.

Jamie Lockhart opened his eyes and looked at her. The candle gave one long beam of light, which traveled between their two faces.

"You are Jamie Lockhart!" she said.

"And you are Clement Musgrove's silly daughter!" said he.

Then he rose out of his bed.

"Good-by," he said. "For you did not trust me, and did not love me, for you wanted only to know who I am. Now I cannot stay in the house with you."

And going straight to the window, he climbed out through it and in another moment was gone.

Then Rosamond tried to follow and climbed out after him, but she fell in the dust.

At the same moment, she felt the stirring within her that sent her a fresh piece of news.

And finally a cloud went over the moon, and all was dark night.

5

THE NEXT MORNING, WHEN ROSAMOND CAME TO her senses, she was still lying where she had fallen. This angered her enough, but then from her own bedroom window a head looked out. It was Goat.

"Who are you?" she said.

"Goat," he said.

"Why are you here?"

"I work here," said Goat, "and for the little locket you wear around your neck I will give you some news."

"This locket is all I have left in the world," said the poor girl. "And I already know everything and can learn nothing new."

"Do not be so sad as all that," said Goat, "and I will sing you a song."

Then he gave her a smile, where his teeth showed like a few stars on a cloudy evening, and he sang her the song he had heard her sing:

"The moon shone bright, and it cast a fair light:
'Welcome,' says she, 'my honey, my sweet!
For I have loved thee this seven long year,
And our chance it was we could never meet.'

Then he took her in his armes-two,
And kissed her both cheek and chin,
And twice or thrice he kissed this may
Before they were parted in twin."

But then he had to stop, because her tears made his clothes liable to dampness.

"That is not the news," said Rosamond, "for that is an old story. I will certainly pay you nothing at all for singing it."

"Then I did it for nothing," said Goat, "and it is all the same to me. And now for the same price I will give you the real news, the latest news, the very truth! Only, it lacks rhyme."

"It will not be any better for me," said Rosamond.

"First: your husband is Jamie Lockhart, the bandit of the woods!" cried Goat. "Second: there was wicked murder done in Jamie Lockhart's house in the night! Third: the first man that brings in Jamie Lockhart's head will get a hundred pieces of gold, and the rest will go without! Fourth: the whole world around will be looking for Jamie Lockhart! Fifth: he jumped out the window and left you alone. And sixth: it all went just as she swore it would go, and I will get a suckling pig."

"Just as who swore it would go?" asked Rosamond, for she got a surprise at the end.

"Why, your stepmother, of course," said Goat, and he danced a jig called "Fiddle in the Ditch." "Everything has now worked out to the most perfect fraction of calculation."

"So you work for her!" said Rosamond. "Where have you been all night?"

"Ah! under your bed," said Goat. "And you never looked there. Then by the window, and I saw you wash his face, and I watched you tumble out after him when he told you good-by. And I have been on the lookout ever since, but I do not think he will come back, for what goes out the window seldom returns the same way."

"Leave me!" cried Rosamond. "And let me cry."

So Goat was leaving, but just then a voice said, "Let me out!" And there was the trunk that the Little Harp left, which they had forgotten to throw out after him.

"What did you say?" asked Goat, bending down to put his ear to the top. "Repeat it, please, for I am a little hard of hearing when there is conversation through a trunk."

"Let me out!" said the voice, a bit louder.

So Goat lifted up the lid. And there sat the head of Big Harp, Little Harp's brother, all wrapped up in the blue mud, and just as it came down off the pole in Rodney.

"Will you look what was doing the talking!" cried Goat, and pulled the head out by the hair, holding it up at arm's length so it turned round like a bird cage on a string, and admiring it from all directions.

Poor Rosamond, after one look, fainted again onto the grass, and Goat ran off and left her where she lay.

Setting the head atop his own head, he skipped off down the hill, and he began to kick up his heels to the left and right and cry, "Jamie Lockhart is the bandit of the woods! And the bandit of the woods is Jamie Lockhart!"

But there was no time at all before the drums began to sound all around, north, south, east, and west, until the very leaves of the trees chattered with it. The branches slowly parted everywhere, and a multitude of faces looked out between.

Clement heard Goat's cry floating out of the forest, saying "Jamie Lockhart is the bandit of the woods! And the bandit of the woods is Jamie Lockhart!"

"Now there must be a choice made," he said. He walked away into the forest and placed the stones in a little circle around him and sat unheeded in the pine grove.

"What exactly is this now?" he said, for he too was concerned with the identity of a man, and had to speak, if only to the stones. "What is the place and time? Here are all possible trees in a forest, and they grow as tall and as great and as close to one another as they could ever grow in the world. Upon each limb is a singing bird, and across this floor, slowly and softly and forever moving into profile, is always a beast, one of a procession, weighted low with his burning coat, looking from the yellow eye set in his head." He stayed and looked at the place where he was until he knew it by heart, and could even see the changes of the seasons

The head of Big Harp

come over it like four clouds: Spring and the clear and separate leaves mounting to the top of the sky, the black flames of cedars, the young trees shining like the lanterns, the magnolias softly ignited; Summer and the vines falling down over the darkest caves, red and green, changing to the purple of grapes and the Autumn descending in a golden curtain; then in the nakedness of the Winter wood the buffalo on his sinking trail, pawing the ice till his forelock hangs in the spring, and the deer following behind to the salty places to transfix his tender head. And that was the way the years went by.

"But the time of cunning has come," said Clement, "and my time is over, for cunning is of a world I will have no part in. Two long ripples are following down the Mississippi behind the approaching somnolent eyes of the alligator. And like the tenderest deer, a band of copying Indians poses along the bluff to draw us near them. Men following men down the Mississippi, hoarse and arrogant by day, wakeful and dreamless by night at the unknown landings. A trail leads like a tunnel under the roof of this wilderness. Everywhere the traps are set. Why? And what kind of time is this, when all is first given, then stolen away?

"Wrath and love burn only like the campfires. And even the appearance of a hero is no longer a single and majestic event like that of a star in the heavens, but a wandering fire soon lost. A journey is forever lonely and parallel to death, but the two watch each other, the traveler and the bandit, through the trees. Like will-o'-the-wisps the little blazes burn on the rafts all night, unsteady beside the shore. Where are they even so soon as tomorrow? Massacre is hard to tell from the performance of other rites, in the great silence where the wanderer is coming. Murder is as soundless as a spout of blood, as regular and rhythmic as sleep. Many find a skull and a little branching of bones between two floors of leaves. In the sky is the perpetual wheel of buzzards. A circle of bandits counts out the gold, with bending shoulders more slaves mount the block and go down, a planter makes a gesture of abundance with his riding whip, a flatboatman falls back from the tavern door to the river below with scarcely time for a splash, a rope descends from a tree and curls into a noose. And all around again are the Indians.

"Yet no one can laugh or cry so savagely in this wilderness as to be heard by the nearest traveler or remembered the next year. A fiddle played in a finished hut in a clearing is as vagrant as the swamp breeze. What will the seasons be, when we are lost and dead? The dreadful heat and cold—no more than the shooting star."

So while Clement was talking so long to himself on the lateness of the age, the Indians came closer and found him. A red hand dragged him to his feet. He looked into large, worldly eyes.

"The settlement has come, and the reckoning is here," said Salome. "Punishments and rewards are in order!" And she went out to the woods to look for Jamie Lockhart and have his head, for that was the kind of thing she had wanted to do all her life. So she had her claw shading her sharp eye, but her eye, from thinking of golden glitter, had possibly gotten too bright to see the dark that was close around her now, and while she scanned the sky the bush at her side came alive, and folded her to the ground.

"All I must do is cut off his head," said the Little Harp. "Then I can take his place. Advancement is only a matter of swapping heads about. I could be king of the bandits! Oh, the way to get ahead is to cut a head off!" said the Little Harp. And he looked about for some person to tell that to; but the face that looked back at him was redskinned and surrounded by feathers, and it wore a terrible frown. So the Little Harp was taken in the pose of a head-hunter, with one knee raised and one arm high, with his hand around his sharp knife. Red arms twined around him like a soft net, and off he was borne, held fast in his gesture.

Rosamond, who had fallen on a thorn, eventually felt its prick. She came out of her faint and sat up on the ground.

"Where can I be?" she said, and when she looked behind her and saw the house of the robbers at the end of the lane of cedars, her memory could not collect it all at once, but went slowly up the path, gathering this and that little thing in its sight, until at last it went in at the front door, and she recollected all that had happened. So she began to cry.

"My husband was a robber and not a bridegroom," she said. "He brought me his love under a mask, and kept all the truth hidden from me, and never called anything by its true name, even his name or mine, and what I would have given him he liked better to steal. And if I had no faith, he had little honor, to deprive a woman of giving her love freely."

Weeping made her feel better, and so she went on with it. "Now I am deserted," she said. "I have been sent out of my happiness, even the house has thrown me out the window. Oh," she said, starting to her feet, "if I could only find my husband, I would tell him that he has broken my heart."

Holding out her arms she ran straight into the woods, but before she had gone far, an Indian savage appeared suddenly before her in the mask of a spotty leopard. So for the third time, Rosamond fell down in a faint, and the Indian carried her away.

As for Jamie, he had chosen this time of all the times to finish out his sleep, for he considered it had half been taken away from him the night before. There he lay on the ground under a plum tree, napping away with a smile on his face, while the paths of the innocent Clement and the greedy Salome and the mad Little Harp and the reproachful Rosamond all turned like the spokes of the wheel toward this dreaming hub. If the Indians had not stopped them off, he would have been dead three or four times and accused and forgiven once before he woke up. But while he still slept, the savages found him first, and lifted him, heavy with sleeping like a child, onto one of the little Asiatic horses they had, and tied him down with their sharp threads.

The Indian in the leopard mask

Then, to destroy the body of the maiden that had been contaminated, the Indians set fire to the robbers' house, and it went up in five points of red flame. The raven flew out over the treetops and was never seen again, and the forest was filled with the cry of the dogs.

So there they all ended in the Indian camp. One by one the savages had captured them all.

All, that is, except Goat, who, having turned the head of Big Harp loose on the world, could not get enough of running through the woods with it, crying, "Bring in his head! Bring in his head! A price is on his head!" In this manner he escaped, for the Indians searched in devious and secret ways only, in their revenge, and with his cry he shot straight through their fancy net.

Now this was a small camp, in a worn-away hollow stirred out by the river, the shell of a whirlpool, called the Devil's Punch Bowl. The rays of the sun had to beat down slantwise, and the Indians' dogs ran always in circles. So there all the young Indians danced at sunset, and the old Indians sat about folded up like women, with their withered knees by their ears. The small-boned ponies fed on the brown grass, and their teeth cut away with a scallopy sound. The yellow fires burned at regular places, and out of the cloud of smoke which hung in the shape of a flapping crow over the hut of the Chief, the odor of the dead blew round, for the venerated ancestors of the tribe were stretched inside upon their hammocks and gently swayed by the Autumn wind.

On this night, all the Indians, being very tired from their long day's work of revenge, fell back upon their mats and went to sleep with the sun. Having first made sure that all the prisoners were tied and left inside a hut, they put off punishing them until another day, for sleep had come to be sweeter than revenge.

So by the time the moon rose, Goat was running and scampering about the huts where the prisoners were tied, making no more noise than a swarm of gnats.

"Here are these great strong bullies tied up," he said, "and I am free."

So he looked in first one hut and then the other.

Poor Rosamond, on the point of fainting, and very hungry, was waiting for her death. Believing by now that she would never see her husband again, she thought dearly of that old life, and was fond of even the disguise he had worn.

"Now that I know his name is Jamie Lockhart, what has the news brought me?" she asked, and had only to look down at the ropes that bound her to see that names were nothing and untied no knots.

Goat, passing by and hearing her tears, recognized her at once by the sound, and popping his head through the chink in the door, he said, "Good evening, why are you crying?"

"Oh, I have lost my husband, and he has lost me, and we are both tied up to be killed in the morning," she cried.

"Then cry on," said Goat, "for I never expect to hear a better reason."

"Perhaps he is already dead," said Rosamond. "For I cannot believe, if he were alive, that he would not come and find me, whether he is tied up or not."

"If he is not dead now, he is as good as dead," said Goat. "Is there anything that I could do for you in his place?"

"Let me out!" begged Rosamond.

"Well, now," said Goat, "what will you give me?"

"Anything!" said Rosamond. "Do you want my locket?"

"No," said Goat. "I don't always want a locket."

"Then what do you want?"

"Will you let me come and live with you in the robbers' house when Jamie Lockhart and all the robbers are dead?"

"Yes," said Rosamond, "I will."

"And will you cook the meat and serve me at the same table where they sat?"

"Yes, yes," said Rosamond. "But let me out now."

"And will you let me come sleep in your little bed, and be my wife?" asked Goat.

"Yes!" cried Rosamond, and it was lucky for her she did not have to learn to tell a lie there on the spot, but already knew how.

"Then I ask no money," said Goat, and he stuck his little hand inside the door and lifted the latch. Then he came and bit the knots in two.

"Wait for me in the robbers' house," he whispered. "Have the kettle on the fire, and the bed turned down."

So Rosamond was free, and stole away to the woods.

Next Goat went by the hut where Salome was kept, and putting his head to the crack he said, "Good evening, why are you crying?"

"I am not crying!" said Salome, and indeed she was not, or anything like it. "Be gone! I need no one!"

So Goat let her stay.

Then, passing by the hut where Jamie and the Little Harp and the rest of the robbers were kept, Goat stopped and listened and heard a great quarreling. It was Jamie and the Little Harp, and the rest of the robbers were stretched out like the dead and snoring, and slept through the whole affair, for they were as tired as the Indians.

But at that moment the Little Harp said, "Quiet! I hear something just outside the door."

"What do you hear?" asked Jamie.

"I think it is a woodchuck," said the Little Harp, "from the scuffle in the leaves."

"Good evening," said Goat through the crack, in a voice like a woodchuck's. "The woodchucks have come, to see the big fight."

"What big fight?" said the Little Harp.

"Yours," said Goat. Then he did a little step, and Harp said, "Listen! I heard something running, and I think it is a squirrel."

"Good evening," said Goat through the crack, in the affected voice of a squirrel. "The squirrels have come, to see the big fight."

"What big fight?" said the Little Harp.

"Yours," said Goat.

Then he gave a grunt like a boar, and a hiss like a snake, and a sniff like a fox, and a scratch like a bear, and a howl like a wildcat, and a roar like a lion.

"Good evening," he said, roaring, "we have come to see the big fight."

"The Lord help us," said the Little Harp to Jamie, "but the fight must be going to be monstrous! I never knew there was even a lion about!"

"What fight?" asked Jamie, for he had heard none of this.

"Ours!" said the Little Harp. "Only we are tied up and can't get at it."

Just then Goat put his head in the crack.

"Good evening," he said, "could I do anything for you?"

"Here is our chance," said the Little Harp to Jamie. "This fellow works for me, and if I pay him enough, he will lift the latch and come in and untie us, and we can get at it."

"The sooner the better then," said Jamie, "for this might as well be gotten over with."

So the Little Harp promised Goat half of the reward money for Jamie's head and a brace of fighting turkeys, and Goat came in and untied him.

"So far, so good," said the Little Harp. "Now keep the enemy still tied for a bit, as I wish to do some work on him without the trouble I had before."

Then he pulled out a knife and walked up to Jamie and measured how far he was around the neck.

"The price is on this part of him," remarked the

Little Harp to Goat, "so I think I will take the head and let the rest go, for this is all we need." And he was just about to cut off his head.

"Wait! Or we will have one head too many," said Goat. "At this very moment, the head that came out of your little trunk is resting on a new-cut pole in Rodney square under the name of Jamie Lockhart, the bandit of the woods."

"The Big Harp would kill me for that, if he were alive," said the Little Harp. "For he was very vain of his name, and after every robbery we ever did together, he would look back over his shoulder at what he had done, and call, 'We are the Harps!' as we ran to the woods."

"Don't cry for that," said Goat, "but look at the gold I have got. They said, 'Who killed Jamie Lockhart, and wrapped up his head so nice and brought it in?' and I said, 'I did.' And they trotted out the sack of gold before you could say 'Nebuchadnezzar.'" So he held up the gold.

"So far, so good," said the Little Harp. "Now turn the sum over to me." And he lifted the bag of gold out of Goat's hand.

"But it is my brain's money!" cried Goat.

"It is my brother's head!" cried the Little Harp.

"But I am Jamie Lockhart, the bandit of the woods!" cried Jamie. "This is all a madness!"

"Let it be untangled at once," said the Little Harp, sitting down between them and putting his great hand to his tiny head. "Now, first—I take back my words of yesterday—rash, headstrong words. And so you, sir, my good stranger, are *not* Jamie Lockhart, the bandit of the woods. And second, that is not your own head you are wearing, and third, I don't want it, and fourth, I won't have it."

"But I am Jamie Lockhart, the bandit of the woods!" cried Jamie. "Not a man in the world can say I am not who I am and what I am, and live!"

"Yes they can!" said the Little Harp. "I tell you you are not and never will be. I stand here and say Jamie Lockhart, the bandit of the woods, is dead, and his head rides a stick-horse in Rodney square, and here hot in my hand is the money that his life was worth."

"Now the time has come to fight!" cried Jamie.

There was a shy little smile on the Little Harp's face at that, and he said, "What's more, there is no more Big Harp any more, for his head is gone, and the Little Harp rules now. And for the proof of everything, I'm killing you now with my own two hands." With this, he rushed upon Jamie in full confidence. But Jamie leaped up and burst his ropes with one great strong breath, and caught him in the middle of the air.

And this time Jamie had no hesitations about what to do, but went for the Little Harp with all his might, and that was needed.

Goat, seeing that the fight had started at last, butted out through the door and sat on the roof of the hut like an owl. In the next moment out rolled the two men through the door after him, and they tore the turf and leveled whatever tree they fought under, until now and again an Indian woke up and quivered in his bed.

They fought the whole night through, till the sun came up. At last, just as the Little Harp had his knife point in Jamie's throat, and a drop of blood stood on it, Jamie pulled out his own little dirk and stopped the deed then and there.

The Little Harp, with a wound in his heart, heaved a deep sigh and a tear came out of his eye, for he hated to give up his life as badly as the deer in the woods.

So Jamie left him dead on the ground, tied in his own belt the reward that had been offered for his life, and started off a free man.

When the Indians gathered round and found themselves cheated of trying the two bandit leaders in court—one being already dead, and one being free— their fury was without bounds. So they rushed upon the rest of the robber band, the lazy ones who were still snoring in their places, and scalped them every one.

Then the drums began to beat, and to avenge the death of the Indian maiden, they sent for the beautiful girl they had captured to appear before their circle.

But Salome, in her hut, heard them coming for Rosamond, and she cried out and said, "What beautiful girl are you looking for? I am the most beautiful!" For she was jealous even of not being chosen the victim.

"What of the young girl with the golden hair?" said the Indians.

"She is dead!" cried Salome. Her voice rose to a great shout. "She is dead! I saw her die!"

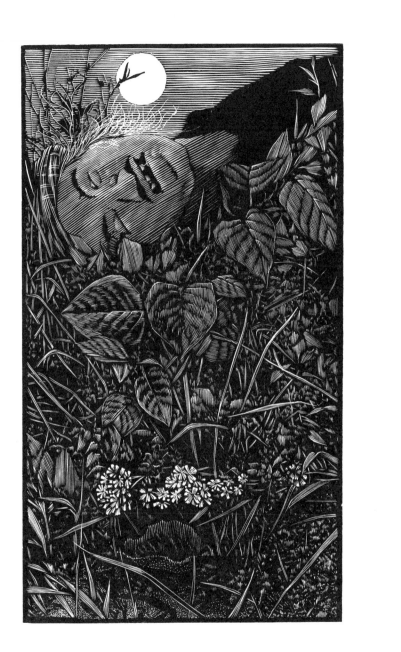

The death of Little Harp

Then a great groan went up from Clement, who heard her from where he was bound in his hut. For like Rosamond, he believed her at last, when the day came.

"Alas!" said the Indians, sad and cheated once more. "How did the beautiful girl meet this early death?"

"She ran from the hut, escaping in the night," said Salome. "And a great spotted leopard came and carried her off between his teeth!"

So they went and looked, and sure enough, Rosamond was gone and there was no sign of her at all. "It must have been a leopard," they said.

"Now, will you choose me?" Salome asked.

So the Indians led her out into their circle and stood her up before them.

But before they could say anything at all to her, Salome opened her mouth and gave them a terrible, long harangue that made them put their fingers in their ears. She told them all she knew.

"It is the command of our Chief," they told her, "that you be still."

"I won't be still!" said she, and told them everything over.

"It is the command of the sun itself," they told her, "that you be still." But though they approached her, they did not lay their hands upon her, for she seemed dangerous to them.

"No one is to have power over me!" Salome cried, shaking both her fists in the smoky air. "No man, and none of the elements! I am by myself in the world."

Then they looked at one another. And Clement,

from where he was bound, saw the sad faces of the Indians, like the faces of feverish children, and said to himself, "The savages have only come the sooner to their end; we will come to ours too. Why have I built my house, and added to it? The planter will go after the hunter, and the merchant after the planter, all having their day."

"The sun will lay his hand upon you," said the Indian Chief himself to Salome, speaking from the center of the circle. "The sun asks worship."

"The sun cannot punish me," cried Salome. "Punishment is always the proof. Why, I could punish the sun if I wished! For I have seen your sun with a shadow eating it, and I know it for a weak thing in the Winter, like all the rest of life!"

"She would throw mud on the face of the sun," said the Indians, drawing their circle in upon Salome and their hands lifting with their tomahawks, but not touching her.

Salome only laughed the more. "I can punish your sun if I wish!" she cried. "I will tell the sun now to stand still, and it will stand still!" And she threw back her head and called, "Sun! Stand where you are!"

Then anger came over all the faces of the Indians and dissolved the weariness that was there, and up sprang the young son of the Chief, bounding forward to the center of the circle. His hand went up for the first time above his father's, and he gave a command in a voice as strong as a buffalo's.

"You dared to command the sun!" he cried. "And you must dance for it."

Then his father raised his arms too, and all the other savages spread their arms high like the branches of trees, and moved inward.

"Dance!" they said. "If you dare to command the sun, dance!"

So Salome began to dance, whether she wanted to or whether she didn't, and the Indian Chief said, "If you stand still before the sun obeys you and stands still likewise, it is death for you."

So Salome danced and shouted, "Sun, retire! Go back, Sun! Sun, stand still!"

But it went on as it always had, and the Indian Chief said, "One like you cannot force him, for his home is above the clouds, in a tranquil place. He is the source of our tribe and of every thing, and therefore he does not and will not stand still, but continues forever."

So Salome danced. Out went her arms, hop went her bony feet, in and out went her head on her neck, like a hen that flies before the hawk. Around the fire they drummed her, and she danced till her limbs seemed all red-hot. One by one she cast off her petticoats, until at the end she danced as naked as a plucked goose, and faster and faster, until the dance was raveled out and she could dance no more. And still the sun went on as well as ever.

There she stood, blue as a thistle, and over she fell, stone dead.

"What man," said the Indian Chief, "owns the body of this woman?"

"I do," said Clement. "I own her body."

117

"Then take it and go free," said the Chief. Pity ran through all the grooves of his brown face.

So for the second time in his life, Clement was not held for a prisoner by the Indian savages, or put to death. The body of Salome was tied to a bony pony, and Clement was given the rope to lead it away.

Now Jamie all this time had been hiding in a gully, biding his time, and, by felling Indians, making his way through the woods to the rear of the huts. Then there was Goat beside him.

"Where are you going?" said Goat. "For I thought you were free and away."

"I am going where my wife is a prisoner, and get her and take her home if I lose my life for doing it," said Jamie. "For when I went off and left her, I had no idea what a big thing would come of it."

"Ah, but you are too late now," said Goat. "She believes you are dead, and is untied already and gone, and now she has promised to marry another husband. For seeing that you would be a dead man and I a live one, she has chosen me."

At that, Jamie half pulled out his little dirk again, but then he showed his teeth in a laugh. "It is too bad," said he, "that she did not tell you that she burns every piece of meat she sticks over the fire, and cannot sew a straight seam, and that her feet are cold in the bed at night."

"She did not," cried Goat. "It is a pity the cheating that goes on in a bargain."

"She is a noted liar," said Jamie, "that is known as

far as the Bayou Pierre. And I only keep her because I I stole her in the first place and have a soft sentiment about it.''

"Still," said Goat, "I have something to expect for the work I have done. My tongue is hanging out from all my efforts."

"So it is," said Jamie.

"And it is not as if both my employers were not freshly dead and I will not have any more work," said Goat, "unless I scratch up something for myself."

"That is true," said Jamie.

"If there were such a thing as any reward money to be had," said Goat, "I should almost rather have that than either work or a wife."

"Hold out your hand, then," said Jamie, and he put the bag of gold into it. "That is the reward for a bandit's life, for the bandit's life is done with, though I must say I think it was worth more."

"Well and good," said Goat. "And know that this will be used to allow me to rest for a while, and then to buy a black cook, give all my sisters in marriage, and to enrich my mother in every way."

Then Jamie went on alone, and on foot, for his horse had been taken away from him and he had not found him yet. He went on and on and at last he came to the lane of the cedars.

But when he reached the place where the robbers' house had been, there was only a heap of cinders, with the long smoke cloud hanging over it. Then he searched and found the small bones lying in the embers, that had been the Indian maiden's. So he thought a trick had been played upon him after all, and that Rosamond was dead. And he ran wild through the woods.

6

Rosamond, in the meanwhile, was as lost as she could be in the woods, and making her way along the Old Natchez Trace. And of everybody she met she would ask the same question: "Have you seen Jamie Lockhart?" And they all said, "No indeed."

She was sadly tattered and torn, and tired from sleeping in hollow trees and keeping awake in the woods, so that she would not have been recognized by her own father, who, indeed, thought she was dead, carried off by a panther and eaten up.

So on one of the days she saw a man sleeping in the woods, and heard the sound of his horse near-by. And when she got up to the man, he had such a stature, though lying on the ground, she thought it would certainly be Jamie Lockhart having a nap. So she went up and touched him. But when he turned over he was the wrong man.

"You may wonder why I am taking a nap here in the middle of the day," the man said at once, sitting up and pulling the straws out of his hair. "Well, I can soon satisfy you as to that."

"Then do," said Rosamond, sitting down beside him, for she had had curiosity before and would have it again, and she thought, "Who knows? He may have seen my husband, since something knocked his wind out."

"I am a mail rider, an anonymous mail rider," said the tall man, "and over yonder is the mail to prove it, tied to the saddle and as safe as a church, for everybody gets out of the way when I come past. But I have just come from an adventure with the grandfather of all alligators, which you may or may not have met as you came along."

"Never an alligator did I see," said Rosamond, "though I saw a monstrous big fish look out of the lake as I passed by, which bared his fangs and whistled at me."

"Oh, but the alligator was worse than the fish," said the mail rider. "I have seen the fish. There he came, the alligator, waltzing as pretty as you please down between the sides of the Old Natchez Trace, and as long as anything you have ever seen come out of the water, ships and all. The first thing he did when he saw me coming was open his mouth, and I was riding so fast, so very fast, bent on my duty, that there was nothing to do but ride on, straight in the front door. And he clicked the latch and shot the bolt behind me."

"That was bad luck for Sunday," said Rosamond.

"And there were two other travelers in there already," said the mail rider.

"Did one have yellow hair?" asked Rosamond, for she thought that this was where Jamie Lockhart might have been, the victim of this fate.

"No, they were both too old for that," said the mail rider. "They never said a word. Luckily, I had just the moment before felt a desire for some persimmons, and not wishing to stop long enough to pick them one by one, I stuck out my hand as I rode by and pulled up the next persimmon tree by the roots. So I took it with me and ate from that as I went along. So, I propped the old alligator's mouth open with the persimmon tree."

"Were the persimmons ripe yet?" asked Rosamond.

"Hold back, madame," said the mail rider. "For this is what happened to me and not to you, and it is my business whether the persimmons were ripe or not. So the old grandfather said, 'Aaaaarh!' and gave such a horrid switch to his tail that his back teeth were rolling like thunder, but I didn't change my tune just because he didn't like it. First I took a good look around by the light of day, it being my first sight of an alligator's mouth from that direction. But teeth, teeth, nothing but teeth! I have never ridden my horse by so many teeth before. But when I said 'Gidyap!' and started back to civilization, do you know what happened?"

"Did he swallow you?" asked Rosamond.

"No indeed. How would he dare?" asked the mail rider. "But the persimmons on the persimmon tree were green, it being not quite late enough in the year to prop up an alligator with that kind of tree. And

125

there, the way they draw up a mouth, they had drawn up the creature's mouth like a moneybag before I could ride as far as from me to you. So I couldn't get out and there I was."

"Did you make a noise?" asked Rosamond. "I have often thought that would discourage an alligator who was swallowing people down."

"Noise was not the practical thing in that predicament," said the mail rider. "There was still left the tiniest, smallest hole you can imagine where I could see out into the world, and so dark it was inside that I saw the stars in the daytime. So I steered him around by the Big Dipper, with the other two fellows helping, all the way from East to West, and made him face full on the hot sun. And down it shone and ripened the persimmons on one side of the tree, while I built a little fire and ripened them on the other, though I had to use the merest bit of mail for the kindling, the other two fellows having nothing of use on them. So as soon as the persimmons were ripe, the alligator's mouth undrew, and I whipped up my horse and took my departure. And I suppose the others followed, though I never looked back to see. But the adventure has tired me, and I was lying down for a moment when you discovered me here."

"I am sorry to have disturbed your rest," said Rosamond. "But I wanted only to ask you a question. Have you seen Jamie Lockhart?"

At this, the mail rider jumped white to his feet and sat down whiter still. "Jamie Lockhart the ghost?" he said.

"God in Heaven, is he a ghost now?" cried Rosamond.

"I should say he is," said the rider. "And has been."

"Ah, how do you know?" cried Rosamond. "Tell me quickly what has happened."

"First, take a bite to eat," said he, and brought out a little napkin of meat and biscuit. And Rosamond, who had never been hungrier, accepted with thanks.

"To begin at the beginning," said the rider, "I won't say who I am. For that is a secret."

"Too much of this secrecy goes on in the world for my happiness," said Rosamond. "But skip over the dark spot and get on to the light."

"Where was I?" said he.

"You were saying that Jamie Lockhart is a ghost!" cried Rosamond. "How do you know?"

"That is easy to answer," said the mail rider. "I know he is a ghost because I made him one myself, with these very hands you see here holding the biscuit." Then he sighed and said, "But that was in the old days, and I dare say you don't believe that I was ever that big a figure in the world."

"Tell me the story straight," said Rosamond, "and leave yourself out."

"Oh, we had a terrible battle, Jamie Lockhart and I," said he. "It lasted through three nights running, and when we were through they had to get the floor and the roof switched back to their places, for we had turned the house inside out. Dozens and dozens of seagulls were dead, that had flown in off the river and got caught in the whirlwind of the fight. Hundreds of people were watching, and got their noses sliced off too, for standing too close."

"It's a wonder Jamie Lockhart did not kill you," said Rosamond.

"Do you know the reason?" said the mail rider. "It's because I killed him first. I beat him to a pulp—there was nothing left but the juice."

"I can hardly believe he would have let you," said Rosamond.

"The very next morning I saw his ghost," said the mail rider, "for it came in and said good morning to me, and not a scratch on it."

"And have you seen it since?" she said.

"At this very spot and at this very time yesterday," said he. "Why didn't you tell me in the first place that you were looking for Jamie Lockhart's ghost? For I know it well."

"Which direction was it going in?" asked Rosamond anxiously.

"In this very direction," said he. "I was riding along, and there it was, sitting on a gate. I knew that shape of a fine tall man with that illusion of yellow hair and that pretence of a coat tied on it like a cape. And I smelled the sulphur when it said, 'A nice evening for August.'

"So I said, 'Good evening, Jamie Lockhart's ghost.'

"And it smiled, and there were its same teeth.

"I asked it what it had been doing since the last time I saw it.

"'Sitting on a gate,' said it.

"'And are you unhappy or looking for anything?' says I, for I knew how ghosts are.

Rosamond, pregnant with twins

"'Yes,' says it, 'I'm looking for my red horse Orion, have you seen its ghost flying along without its rider?'

"So I made haste to tell it where I had seen the horse, which had indeed passed me like the devil himself, going south, and the ghost said it was likely to be waiting by the old tavern door in Rodney's Landing, the very spot where we had had the fight and I had killed it. So the ghost went along with me till we got to Rodney, talking very amiable, but of course nothing we said was true. Though sure enough, there was the horse waiting like a tame mouse beside the tavern door. So it jumped on its back and off it went simply rising into the air, and said it was going to the New Orleans port for the purpose of taking a boat."

"Oh, I must prevent that," said Rosamond. "And you must take me along with you today and give me a ride. For I have a message for Jamie Lockhart from another world."

"Is it a message from out of the past for the old ghost?" asked the mail rider.

"No, it is from out of the future," said Rosamond. And she put it to him, "Did you ever before hear of an old ghost that was going to be a father of twins next week?"

"Oh!" he said. "Ghosts are getting more powerful every day in these parts. But ghost or no ghost, I wish now I had punched him in the nose, even if there was nothing there, for his rascality."

And he set Rosamond up on his horse in front of him, and laid on the whip, and they rode away down the Trace.

So while they were going along, some bandits rushed down upon them from a clump of pine trees, and told them to stop in their tracks for they meant to rob the mail.

"Pass on!" cried the mail rider. "This lady is soon to become a mother."

So the bandits lifted up their black hats to Rosamond and passed on up the Trace.

At the end of his run, he put her down, and Rosamond thanked him for his favors.

"Now, tell me your real name," said she, "for I must know who it is I had to thank, for the way you have aided a poor deserted wife that is looking for her ghost of a husband."

At this request, the mail rider turned all red like the sunset, but at last he said, "Tell no one, but I am none other than Mike Fink! It would be outrageous if this were known, that the greatest flatboatman of them all came down in the world to be a mail rider on dry land. It would sound like the end of the world! Don't breathe it to a soul that you saw me this way, and you yourself must forget the disgrace as early as you can."

"How on earth did it happen?" asked Rosamond.

"It was enemies," said Mike Fink. "Men jealous of me. They found out that one day, after many years of heroism, I allowed myself to be cheated out of three little sacks of gold and a trained bird, and so they threw me out. All of them jumped on me at one time and it lasted a week, but they sent me up out of the river. They left me for dead on a sand bar in the Bayou Pierre. And so I came to this."

"Out of my gratitude to you, I will tell no one of your true identity," Rosamond promised. "And good luck to you. May you be restored to your proper place."

As a matter of fact, Rosamond told everyone she met, since she was not able to keep silent about it, but no one believed her, and so no harm was done.

Mike Fink rode away saying, "I will have to ride all night to make up for the deed of kindness I have done, and will probably be set upon by the bandits, who are waiting for my return trip when I have no shield before me, and be murdered for it."

But he was not, and in the end he did get back on the river and his name was restored to its original glory. And it is a good thing he never knew that he helped to restore the bride to a live and flourishing Jamie Lockhart, or that would have broken his heart in two.

So Rosamond went on, and by dint of begging one mail rider after another, and trotting upon one white pony after another black horse, she made her way clear to New Orleans.

The moment she reached the great city she made straight for the harbor.

The smell of the flapping fish in the great loud marketplace almost sent her into a faint, but she pressed on bravely along the water front, looking twice at every man she met, even if he looked thrice back at her, and at last she came to where a crowd of gentlemen and sailors were embarking on a great black ship going to Zanzibar. And sure enough, there in the middle, and taller than all the rest like a corn-stalk in the cottonfield, was Jamie Lockhart, waving good-by to the shore.

"Jamie Lockhart!" she cried.

So he turned to see who it was.

"I came and found you!" she cried over all their heads.

Then he took his foot off the gangplank and came down and brought her home, not failing to take her by the priest's and marrying her on the way. And indeed it was in time's nick.

So in the Spring, Clement went on a trip from Rodney's Landing to New Orleans, and was walking about.

New Orleans was the most marvelous city in the Spanish country or anywhere else on the river. Beauty and vice and every delight possible to the soul and body stood hospitably, and usually together, in every doorway and beneath every palmetto by day and lighted torch by night. A shutter opened, and a flower bloomed. The very atmosphere was nothing but aerial spice, the very walls were sugar cane, the very clouds hung as golden as bananas in the sky. But Clement Musgrove was a man who could have walked the streets of Bagdad without sending a second glance overhead at the Magic Carpet, or heard the tambourines of the angels in Paradise without dancing a step, or had his choice of the fruits of the Garden of

Eden without making up his mind. For he was an innocent of the wilderness, and a planter of Rodney's Landing, and this was his good.

So, holding a bag of money in his hand, he went to the docks to depart, and there were all the ships with their sails and their flags flying, and the seagulls dipping their wings like so many bright angels.

And as he was putting his foot on the gangplank, he felt a touch at his sleeve, and there stood his daughter Rosamond, more beautiful than ever, and dressed in a beautiful, rich white gown.

Then how they embraced, for they had thought each other dead and gone.

"Father!" she said. "Look, this wonderful place is my home now, and I am happy again!"

And before the boat could leave, she told him that Jamie Lockhart was now no longer a bandit but a gentleman of the world in New Orleans, respected by all that knew him, a rich merchant in fact. All his wild ways had been shed like a skin, and he could not be kinder to her than he was. They were the parents of beautiful twins, one of whom was named Clementine, and they lived in a beautiful house of marble and cypress wood on the shores of Lake Pontchartrain, with a hundred slaves, and often went boating with other merchants and their wives, the ladies reclining under a blue silk canopy; and they sailed sometimes out on the ocean to look at the pirates' galleons. They had all they wanted in the world, and now that she had found her father still alive, everything was well. Of course, she said at the end, she did sometimes miss the house in the wood, and even the rough-and-tumble of their old life when he used to scorn her for her curiosity. But the city was splendid, she said; it was the place to live.

"Is all this true, Rosamond, or is it a lie?" said Clement.

"It is the truth," she said, and they held the boat while she took him to see for himself, and it was all true but the blue canopy.

Then the yellow-haired Jamie ran and took him by the hand, and for the first time thanked him for his daughter. And as for him, the outward transfer from bandit to merchant had been almost too easy to count it a change at all, and he was enjoying all the same success he had ever had. But now, in his heart Jamie knew that he was a hero and had always been one, only with the power to look both ways and to see a thing from all sides.

Then Rosamond prepared her father a little box lunch with her own hands. She asked him to come and stay with them, but he would not.

"Good-by," they told each other as the wind filled the sails for the voyage home.

"God bless you."

The Robber Bridegroom